QUARTIER PERDU

And Other Stories

SEAN O'BRIEN

Also by the same author
THE SILENCE ROOM

First published in Great Britain in 2018 by Comma Press.
www.commapress.co.uk

Many of the stories in this collection were written to be read at Phantoms
at the Phil, an event held at the Newcastle Literary and Philosophical
Society Library at Christmas and Midsummer.

'Change for Low Rixham' was first published as chapbook by Enchiridion (2011).
'Certain Measures' appeared in Beta Life: Stories from an A-Life Future, ed. Ra Page
and Martyn Amos (Comma Press, 2014). 'Ex Libris' appeared in Lemistry: A
Celebration of the Work of Stanislaw Lem, ed. Ra Page (Comma Press, 2011).
'Lovely' appeared in the Newcastle Journal and in Platform. 'Quartier Perdu' was
broadcast on BBC Radio 4. 'Story Time' appeared in Bio-Punk: Stories from the
Far Side of Research, ed. Ra Page (Comma Press, 2014). 'Swan, 1914' appeared in
Litmus: Short Stories from Modern Science, ed. Ra Page (Comma Press, 2011).

A CIP catalogue record of this book is available from the British Library.

ISBN-10 1905583702
ISBN-13 978-1905583706

The publisher gratefully acknowledges the support of Arts Council England

Supported using public funding by
ARTS COUNCIL
ENGLAND

Printed and bound in England by Clays Ltd

QUARTIER PERDU

For Peter Bennet

Contents

I

During an Air-Raid

VICKY FOUND HERSELF STANDING up, peering into her handbag, then closing it again. She paused for a second so that Ray would notice and break off his conversation with Susie, but it was Susie who saw and shifted her gaze to make him look up. It was obvious now.

'I think I'd better go,' Vicky said.

'Well, let's just finish our drinks,' said Ray. He smiled at her tolerantly and lit a cigarette. Susie busied herself with her compact while looking over it at each of them in turn, awaiting developments. The pub had grown quiet, as if interested in the small, squalid crisis as a relief from the larger processes of the war they seemed to be losing.

'I've already finished,' Vicky said. The noise surged back. Ray smiled and spread his arms to encompass both the young women.

'Well, let's get another and after that we can all go.'

'No, really. I'll leave the pair of you to it. It was very noisy in the shelter last night and I've got a headache and I need some sleep. Busy day in the studio tomorrow.' Why was she justifying herself? Ray moved his head from side to side, consideringly, amused. I just work there, turning the knobs, he had said. She used to think he was joking. Same as you, typing scripts. It's nothing to us, really, when you think about it. She couldn't agree. She had thought that with luck she could make him more serious. Susie, of course, presented no such obstacles. Her smug prettiness was all that was the case with her.

'Well, if that's what you want, I suppose you'd best get off then,' said Ray. 'We'll... we'll... I'll... see you tomorrow.'

'I dare say.'

'Goodnight, then, Vicky,' Susie said with a precise, formal smile that accentuated the voracious size of her mouth. She looked like a stranger now. Her lipstick seemed almost black in the muddy light of the bar. Something had been settled. It was as if Susie was already sitting in some other place, a kind of future, confident that soon the desired visitor would arrive and stay, and the redundant one would be gone.

'I'll try to telephone you,' said Ray. But why would he wish to do so in the middle of the night? Surely he would be sleeping, or occupied?

'Take care,' said Vicky. The noise of the room thickened as she pushed through a crowd of soldiers and their girls.

The street was a sudden silence. It was long dark now. The air held an autumn chill. Searchlights quartered the heavens patiently. Perhaps nothing would come tonight. Vicky realised that in her fury of suspicion she had not thought to note the route they'd taken from Broadcasting House. *Surely*, she told herself now, *you must have expected to go home alone?* Ray had a nose for beer and was prepared to walk distances far beyond Fitzrovia to track it down. There were no landmarks in view here among these nondescript nineteenth-century terraces. A taxi might appear, but she would not waste money on it. She set off, hoping to find a main road and a bus.

Street followed blacked-out street, shuttered shops, law offices, garages, builders' yards. The district, anonymous and wholly unfamiliar, seemed deserted, as if everyone had secretly slipped away, revealing a private silence that had always been there. *Keep going*, Vicky told herself. *Something will turn up. And don't think about the pair of them.* There was no point in wondering where the attraction lay: it existed, that was all, and the pair had acted on it, and now she was an embarrassment, a

2

joke almost, rather than the injured party she surely deserved to be. But it was not to be dwelt on, whatever it was Susie could do for Ray that she could not.

When the sirens began she quickened her pace past a little park, past the ruins of a bombed church and its tumbled graveyard which lay next to a secondary school. Beyond that the streets grew somehow barer, more formal, as if their medium was thinning out. There were taller buildings here, Victorian office premises, shuttered and comfortless charitable institutions, the non-committal shop-fronts of dealers in obscure products, and still there was no one else about. She should have stayed at the pub and put up with them. And been humiliated at greater length now the truth had been revealed and she had caught them in a lie which neither of them seemed to have spotted or to care about. They must think her as foolish as themselves. But at least Ray would have known the way back. The click of her heels on the pavement was lonely now.

As she crossed another anonymous junction she heard the thrumming of the bombers approaching up the river. But in the narrow canyon of the streets she could not make out where the river itself lay. Then, sooner than she had expected, there was the sound of an explosion. No sooner had it damped down than there came another and then another, steadily, as though leisurely laying down a path of fire and death across the capital. She froze for a moment and looked up. The searchlight beams moved frantically among the broken cloud, unable to settle on a target for the ack-ack gunners in the parks. She shook her head and went on.

More explosions, still falling in a regular pattern, now four or five seconds apart, and every time nearer. The bombers must be almost overhead. There was a huge blast on the far side of the crossroads, and a warm gust blew against the back of her legs. She looked over her shoulder. The whole street-end was ablaze with blinding phosphorescence. A high wall collapsed in a wave of brick and glass. The familiar smell of ash and sewage followed, but no ambulance sirens or fire-bells approached. The street seemed stunned in the brief aftermath.

Another bomb fell, much closer, enveloping her in its hot breath. The next one would kill her. There was no way off the street, no shelter, barely a doorway. She took off her shoes and began to run, hopelessly, choking in the dust-cloud. *Wait, wait,* she thought. *Not yet. Please. I'm not finished.* Then, to her right, a sign for the Underground appeared. The mesh shutters were half-down, as if abandoned. She ran bent double through the gap into the booking hall and as she did so, the bomb-blast picked her up and threw her across the concourse and against a wall.

*

She could not tell how long she'd been unconscious. The pressure wave had stopped her watch. It should have killed her, she thought. You read about people found sitting around the dinner-table, intact but stone dead, their food untouched, entombed like impoverished Pharaohs with their meagre grave-goods. She lay for a minute, still dazed, looking abstractedly across the concourse at the street. In the station entrance stood a wall of gold-white flame – breathing, flexing, stretching, as if gathering itself, while black cross-hatchings of smoke and ash ran in waves across its supple skin.

It was, she thought, as if the fire was about to *become.* It was entirely silent in the station, a kind of roaring silence in which it seemed the flames stood and looked tigerishly at her. She knew she must get up and get away, but she was half-stunned, concussed, moving with underwater slowness. She pulled herself upright, shaking her head, her hair full of chalky dust and smuts, her suit grey-white with ash, her stockings – a gift from Ray – torn to ribbons, her handbag still somehow over her shoulder, her shoes nowhere to be found.

The heat was intensifying: at any moment the fire would come inside to claim her. She found her way to the top to the escalators. The unmoving wooden treads seemed to plunge off into the dark after a few steps. Not that way. There needed to be a barrier she could close behind her. Beside the escalator was the entrance to the emergency staircase. She opened the heavy iron door: inside lay a descending stone spiral and more darkness. She stepped through and let the door grind shut, took a matchbox from her bag and struck a light. As it flared, her shadow ran away before her down the dim curve. There was an immense thud behind her, as if a great beast had hurled itself at the other side of the iron door. The match-flame shivered and died. She began to make her way down, with one hand on the rail and the other held out before her as if bearing an invisible and sightless torch. For a time she heard the fire slamming itself against the iron door, but after that there was only her breathing.

She counted three hundred before the stairs ended in another door. She pushed it open, thinking this must be one of the deepest lines in the city. In the arched corridor a dim fluorescence lit up the yellowish tiles, and a warm breeze blew the charred pages of a newspaper past her feet. She decided to go left, and moved slowly along the passage until another short flight of steps brought her down on to the platform at the midway point. Here too there was just light to see by, though she couldn't think where it was coming from. JERUSALEM ROAD, the name read. She hadn't heard of it. She supposed it must be disused.

She flinched at the sudden cold underfoot. The place was flooded. The whole track-bed was submerged and a skin of water rippled along the platform. The curving roof of the tunnel ran with the faint light of the water's movement. The

5

whole system must have shorted, so there was no danger of electrocution. And somewhere the mains or the sewers had been breached, and the waters must be making their way down to wherever the very bottom of things lay. It did not seem to growing any deeper here.

She was about to go back into the corridor when a faint illumination swung into view near the mouth of the tunnel – like a lantern, she thought, and imagined railway workers escaping a disaster elsewhere, or searching for survivors. The swaying light seemed muffled. Something made her hesitate to call out. Eventually it emerged – an old lantern, suspended from a pole, mounted on something she could not at first identify – because of course it could not really be there, but that was in fact a boat, a longish craft, low in the dark water, seemingly piled with bundles of sacks or blankets, and steered from the rear by a figure using a single long oar. The whole arrangement struck her as somehow Mediterranean.

The vessel made no sound as it approached along the platform with inches to spare on either side. Thinking it would simply go floating past and disappear into the far tunnel-mouth, Vicky stepped forward and, feeling foolish, put out her arm.

'You,' said the oarsman. 'What is it you want?' She could not see his face. He wore a huge dark hooded coat of sacking. His voice was rusty with age.

'I want to get away,' she said.

'Then you've come to the wrong shop, Missy. Good evening to you.' He made as if to row on, but she came closer.

'Wait. Please. I'm lost.'

'Yes,' said the oarsman, deftly halting the craft with a faint impact on the concrete coping of the platform. 'And what's that to me?'

'Isn't it obvious? I need your help.' She wished he would remove the hood.

'I wouldn't be so sure.'

'Must you be so difficult?' She found it hard to hit the right tone with this strange functionary. He could not be commanded, clearly; neither, it seemed, would he choose to defer.

'Are you coming aboard?' the oarsman asked. She reached out her hand for him to help her.

'Payment first, Miss.' He inclined his head. Vicky felt for her purse.

'I've only got a pound.'

'Then a pound it will be.' He folded the note into the suit of sacking and handed her into the boat. 'Sit in the bow, Miss. You get a better view from there.' She did not like the feel of the piled sacking under her feet, but did as he suggested and went to sit on a cross-board under the lantern. She looked back at the hooded figure, who with the merest gesture propelled the boat along once more. They slid into the tunnel and the darkness came up close once more. The oar moved in near-silence and the tunnel, the labyrinth, the whole place – if it was indeed a place – seemed to be waiting, as the fire had waited, as if the strange vessel might be an augury.

'I'm cold,' she said.

'Wrap yourself in one of those blankets,' came the oarsman's voice.

'I don't like to.'

'Not a matter of liking, is it? There's a war on.' She did as he suggested and tried not to breathe in the rank, bodily smell that came off the coarse material. She felt she might never get rid of the greasy touch of the wool and burlap.

'Has the raid ended?' she asked.

'Not my department,' the oarsman said. 'Down here is me.'

'You mean, at the moment. The water will drain away, or they'll pump it out of the tunnels, won't they? And then your boat won't be needed.' The oarsman shook his head wearily.

'If you say so, Miss.'

'Do you mind if I smoke? I mean, is it safe?'

'Safe? Course it's not safe. But smoke away as you like. Got one to spare? She scrambled back over the heaps of rag and sacking, hating the way they shifted and settled underfoot. She held out the packet of Senior Service.

'Now these I like,' he said. 'Well done.' He reached out a mittened hand and took a cigarette. His nails were long and inky. She made to offer him a light. 'No need.' He seemed to flick his thumb against his forefinger and a thin blue flame appeared. As he leaned to light the cigarette she saw the same light reflected in his eyes, though these too seemed black. *I ought to be more afraid*, she thought.

'You're not wrong,' the steersman remarked. 'But make yourself comfortable.'

'Am I dead?' she asked suddenly.

'Hard to say. Would it matter if you were?'

'Well.' She cast about in her mind. 'Well, it would to me.' The oarsman sniffed.

'That's something, I suppose. Maybe you should give it some more thought.' She went back and sat in the bow, pulling the damp sacking back over her cold legs and feet. There would be rats among it, she supposed. She felt faint, and would have nodded off, but the boat emerged then from the tunnel. It passed alongside a platform whose far side she could not see for the smoke and flame through which she caught glimpses of a vast barrel-vaulted ceiling hung with cages and gibbets. Great roaring furnaces stood on the platform, fed by scurrying figures in black fatigues. She realised that they were fuelling the furnaces with corpses dragged from what looked like luggage carts. A creature in an officer's peaked cap stepped forward to the edge of the platform, scrutinising the boat with invisible eyes. She would have cried out, but a gesture of the oarsman's hand made her keep silent. They passed on into the tunnel again. The black water itself seemed on fire now.

'What is this place?' she hissed at last.

'What indeed? You may well ask,' the oarsman replied. He might have been going on to say something else, but now she did fall asleep.

When next she woke, once more she had no idea of the time elapsed. She heard the oarsman saying, 'You want to see this, Miss.' She looked up as once more they emerged from the tunnel, but this time there was no platform, only a great shallow black lake fed, she saw, by all the tunnels, a great circle of them steadily yet silently emptying their black waters into this vast, oily, circular reservoir that must be at the very bottom, the conclusion, the terminus, the ghost of a railway turntable. If there was a roof, it was too far above to be seen. If there was an exit, it was concealed.

'This is as far as I go,' said the oarsman.

'Now what happens?'

He shrugged. 'You might want to tidy yourself up a bit.'

'You are joking, I take it? Look at me. I'm in rags.'

'It's always worth making an effort.'

'Even down here?'

'That would be my advice. Make the best of it.'

'But why? Why bother? What's the point? There's no one to see or care.'

'Because, my girl, you just have to bloody get on with it. All right? Well, then.' She could not help smiling. She reached into her bag and took out lipstick and compact. When she opened the compact, she winced at her smudged face and the bruise on her cheekbone. She was right. Beyond repair. She spat on her handkerchief and dabbed at the worst of the mess. The oarsman chuckled in a rusty way.

'Excuse me. This is private,' she said. After a time her face looked slightly better, though her hair was still almost white with dust. 'That'll have to do,' she sighed. As she spoke, the mirror in the powder compact seemed to ripple. When it cleared and settled again, she saw the pair of them, in the same seats in the same pub, deep in talk, surrounded by soldiers, but not the same, for these uniforms were field-grey or black. Susie and Ray sat as the table as before with their glasses. They were as much at ease as they had been in her presence earlier that evening, complacent with a sense of rightness and belonging. They had adapted to the altered circumstances. They were realists, of a sort.

She realised she had always known what they would do, to her and in the world at large. *Let them have each other*, she thought, then bent over the water as a wave of nausea ran through her.

'Better out than in,' said the oarsman. 'There's not just you to think about now.'

'I don't know what you mean,' said Vicky.

*

It was a cold grey morning and her breath floated away. There was a smell of recent burning. She lay in a recently-dug grave. Either she'd taken shelter there or been thrown in by a bomb-blast. She tried to climb out but could get no grip on the clay sides. She called for help and after a minute an ARP man appeared at the grave's edge.

'Blimey, darling, let's get you out of there.' He knelt down, extended his black-mittened hands and looked at her steadily when she hesitated to take them. 'It's all right, Miss. You're safe now.' He pulled her up and set her on the grass. 'Can you manage walking?' She nodded and they went across the bombed churchyard with its cracked stones and uprooted skulls on to the street. Her feet were cold and bloody.

In the street a small crowd watched as the firemen rolled

up the hoses and the salvage crew began to pick their way among the wreckage of the pub.

'Must have been a bad night,' she said.

'Well, it was for this lot,' said the ARP man, taking a blanket from a pile in the back of a van, and placing it round her shoulders. 'Direct hit. Poor bastards.'

'Any survivors?'

'Shouldn't think so. Not so far. The rest are laid out in the playground, as much of them as they could find. Miss, you don't want to look at that.' But she had crossed the road to stand in the open gateway of the playground, and the ARP man answered a shouted summons and went off past the wrecked pub.

She counted thirty blanketed bodies. Another helmeted figure approached, his arms outstretched to steer her away. 'I'm looking for someone,' she said, and stepped past him. He seemed to lack the energy to argue the case. She went slowly along the rows, where hands and feet stuck out from under the sacking and blankets, and blood was already drying and fading on the concrete. It was Susie's shoes she recognised, smart black ones with rosettes above the toes. She remembered when Susie first bought them and showed them around the office. And that must be Ray's hand next to her, with its broad thumb and the signet ring that Vicky had always thought vulgar, though she'd never mentioned it. Because Ray was vulgar, really, wasn't he? Unthinking. Uncaring.

Vicky tried to see how it mattered that the pair of them lay here dead, but it escaped her. It was as if she had been away for some time, and now this meant less because there was more to consider. She was tempted to steal Vicky's shoes – no use to her now, were they? She turned and went back through the gate and along the street past the thinning crowd and the grim steady work of the clearing up operation. After a little while she felt sick, but she refused to be ill in the street. She turned a corner and knew now where she was. This was Farringdon Road, with the underground rattling through the cutting below the wall, as if nothing unusual had happened at all. You just had to get on with it.

The Sea-God

HE COULD FEEL THE sun on his back already. As he drank his coffee on the balcony, pleased if a little ashamed to have beaten the Germans in the next room to breakfast today, Acheson could hear Anna and Astrid fussing over the cats down on the wide terrace by the front door. The nursing mothers came down off the mountains with their new kittens, knowing that there would be food, for this was where they themselves had been fed a few months before. After a new litter arrived, Astrid would keep one kitten and dispose of the rest. Anna could be heard lamenting. But it was the only way, she also said.

Acheson did not enquire as to Astrid's methods. Cropped blonde and slightly affectless, she could be seen in the blinding afternoons practising kick-boxing with a bag she'd hung from a mulberry tree. At other times she went about the bay in a small red boat. The twisted ropes fixed at the prow as a buffer against the harbour walls bore a smear of red too, like lipstick. Astrid made Acheson feel frivolous when he sat reading.

Certainly the cat population already outnumbered the humans in the village. The people watched the ferry while the cats watched the people, especially when the fishing boats returned at dawn and evening. And the women kept the whole place ticking over, the black-clad widows glimpsed at work in hidden gardens behind the quay, or staring from dim kitchens while the men lounged importantly by the proprietors' tables under the sunstruck awnings, and the tanned girls home for the holidays went to and fro with trays of beer and octopus.

13

Acheson was a liberal. He understood his guilty part in all of this.

The visitors, to whom all these efforts were devoted, sat blinking in the white-hot light, wondering where they had come to. Like everyone else, discovering there was no mobile phone signal here, they immediately began to watch for the ferry. It called twice a day. In effect the village was an island. There was no road out. If you were a mad German still searching for the abducted General Kneipe you could walk the six kilometres to Platanos along a goat-path, but the scree-slopes of the blinding mountains made this inadvisable. Acheson wasn't much of a walker. He liked to sit and look and write things down. Now that the course he had been teaching – 'Plot, Story: What's the Difference? A Beginner's Guide' – was over and the participants had sailed away, he had given himself a few days simply to do that.

He looked down now and saw Anna, tiny and dark in her long white shift, looking out with a tabby cat in her arms. She spoke to it softly and the cat waited tolerantly, knowing food was in the offing if it played its cards right. Acheson followed Anna's gaze out into the bay. A hundred yards or so offshore, a cylinder of stone or masonry, which Acheson couldn't help thinking of as a head, projected a little above the near-tideless water. In the faint swell, the curve as of shoulders was occasionally revealed for a moment. The stone warned of a submerged rock, he supposed. Nobody moored there, but occasionally village boys swam out and competed to sit on it. They shouldn't do that, not to the sea-god, Acheson thought, and realised he had given it a name. At this distance it was hard to judge how big the head actually was. Naturally it had no face; nevertheless, the mind sought to discover features on the water-weathered drum. Anna turned and saw him looking and waved.

'You should swim, Herr Acheson. This is the best time.'

'Perhaps later. I have work to do.' Anna raised her eyebrows in sympathy and let the cat run away down the steps to the quay. The ferry was rounding the headland.

Strictly speaking, now that the course was over, Acheson had no work to do – not of the contractual, cheque-producing sort. He was, very gently, on his way down. He was unlikely to starve, but he no longer mattered, supposing he ever had. When he woke at 4am, what frightened him was not the prospect of oblivion but his readiness to accept it. It was fair enough. He'd had a good innings, parlaying a middling-to-modest talent on to the bedside tables of the male half of the nation for the best part of twenty years and being wise enough to save the gold when the river ran full of it.

Eventually, and at about the same time, he and the public had begun to grow bored with his work, but readers of thrillers were a loyal bunch and would not wholly desert him for a while yet. After all, they had worked their way into their fifties with his books reliably to hand every summer. Why change now?

This summer there was no book. Rethinking, he said. No one back at home seemed to mind if he just sat here on the balcony and wrote down whatever he randomly observed. Anna and the cat. Astrid disembowelling the heavy bag. The ferry. Caterina, the nineteen-year-old daughter from the restaurant next door, tanned to cinnamon in her tiny red shorts, moving effortlessly among all the glances that followed her. All grist to the mill. And when the week ended he would go home and, well, do something. Something would present itself. For now let there be almost-idleness, while the mind of a man who had once been a poet ticked over, frantic with the scarcely admitted hope that he might surprise himself into long-neglected seriousness or even adventure. *But put that thought away*, he told himself.

He spent the morning in the café at the far end of the village, round by the ferry-landing. As the ferry approached he watched the restaurant boys roll up to stack their blue wheelbarrows with urgent beer and cigarettes for the visitors. Nothing is more important than the blue wheelbarrow, he thought. And you can put that one away, too.

During the siesta he fell asleep reading Tennyson's 'Ulysses', its lines in his head merging with the white silk that seemed to veil the waters in the moment before full dusk:

> Yet all experience is an arch wherethro'
> Gleams that untravelled world, whose margin fades
> For ever and for ever when I move.
> How dull it is to pause, to make an end,
> To rust unburnish'd, not to shine in use!
> As though to breathe were life.

When he awoke, sticky-mouthed and with a headache, he turned and opened the drawer in the bedside table to find some painkillers before realising that he must have moved in his sleep and ended up on the wrong side of the double bed. The drawer on this side contained a Bible and underneath that a small green hardback book, like a journal. He put it down while he found the pills, then went and showered. By the time he returned he had already forgotten the book. Surprised to discover it once more, he took it out on to the balcony.

Below, Anna was preparing a vast bowl of pasta and left-over sauce for the cats, while Astrid sprang two-footed like a dancer at the hanging bag. The sea-god waited in the offing, seeming a little further off amid the late-afternoon glitter of the bay.

Acheson opened the book. The first page was inscribed: *Konrad Wolf, Juni 2008*, and the entries were written in German, in neat, dense black handwriting with dates for each new passage and the names of new places underlined: *Heraklion, Chania, Elafonisi*. The book must have been left behind by accident. Acheson imagined Herr Wolf's pang of disappointment when, far away, he realised he had lost his journal.

But a year had passed and the book was still here. It contained no contact details. The best thing would be to give it to Anna. It was none of Acheson's business. Anna must know it was here in the drawer, surely. The rooms were cleaned daily and then again with especial thoroughness when guests departed. Astrid wielded her broom like a quarterstaff. So perhaps Anna, the boss after all, was indifferent, or else had left it as a curiosity, either of which was odd, but while he considered the alternatives Acheson noted that he had begun to feel a bit possessive about the small green book himself. It might have been a project, perhaps. It was frustrating that his German was far too limited and long ago for him to make much of Wolf's observations. Too bad. He felt like drinking a beer. He went downstairs.

Anna greeted him from her office by the front door.

'Herr Acheson. Good timing!' she said, with her little wizened cat-smile, ushering him into the cool, shaded room where the computer screen shed its glow on piles of paper scattered on the desk. 'You mentioned that you might wish to extend your stay a little beyond the weekend. I must ask, because others may wish to come, what you have decided.'

'I'll stay,' he found himself saying. 'Another week, if that's OK?'

'That is fine. You like our little bay?'

'I do indeed. Very much.' Beyond her shoulder was a bookshelf. She followed his gaze.

'I wonder, would it be possible to borrow your dictionary for a while?'

'But of course. You are reading Goethe, perhaps? Or Hölderlin? He is my favourite.'

'Not quite, I'm afraid.' This was the moment at which to

17

mention Wolf's journal. He let it go. Anna held his gaze, then smiled and shrugged, and reached him the heavy old Duden dictionary in its custard yellow jacket. 'Forgive the dust,' she said.

After he had eaten a dinner of snapper and green beans, Acheson took a carafe of chilled white wine up to his room. Dusk was approaching, the blue sea-horizon softening and vanishing into the sky before finally it would re-emerge for a moment like a firm black line just before dark. He could hear the goat-bells in the stony pastures above and behind him. He moved the little table over into the space between the open French windows and arranged the lamp and his notebook. Then he took the journal from the drawer.

He awoke with a stiff neck, lying back at an awkward angle in the white plastic chair. It was half-past three, a little before dawn, and now he was completely, uselessly awake. He left the house quietly, watched by a cat at the corner of the stairs, crossed the little courtyard and descended to the quay. Among the faint agitations of the water, phrases from Konrad Wolf's journal drifted back to him. He sat on the edge with his feet a few inches above the water and lit a cigarette.

Konrad Wolf had pretensions. Not to mention psychiatric problems.

There are many ways to the land of the dead, the old
    song says,
And you will find your own,
Be in no doubt.' Who doubts it, dearest Sappho?
Does not every day confirm it?
But such a message falls only lightly
On the ears of the living. The fisherman
Home on the ocean since childhood
Is deafened and no longer hears the voice of the waves.
But today my heart was wonderfully startled. Listen!

Wolf had begun by inscribing this stanza from Mörike, a poet unknown to Acheson, who found he liked it less than the Tennyson. Allowing for the obvious defects of his attempt to translate it, the poem's fatalism seemed inert. As far as he knew, Sappho never went anywhere, certainly not into the unknown world beyond the Pillars of Hercules at the mouth of the Mediterranean. She just stayed at her island academy for young ladies and taught, he seemed to remember. As to Wolf, did he just like the noise of the thing, the Mörike, which was admittedly seductive in the original, or did he think he had a reason for sharing the poet's sense of doom? And why did he add a dismissive quotation from Nietzsche commenting on Mörike's poems: 'sickly-sweet whimsy and tinkle-tinkle'? Even Acheson could tell there was more to Mörike than that.

He suddenly felt too tired to consider the matter further. He stared out into the dark sea while finishing his cigarette. As he rose to go, he heard a faint sound out on the water. It came again and he recognised it as oars. He went back up the steps to the terrace and watched. In the first glimmer of dawn the red boat came gliding in, its outboard motor tilted up above the water. The rower was Astrid, stroking effortlessly and near-soundlessly, and in the back of the boat sat Caterina, her brown legs drawn up to her chin, staring down at the covered shape in the bottom of the vessel.

As Astrid slowed their movement, Caterina came lightly forward and stepped on to the jetty, holding a painter which she looped through an iron ring. Astrid brought the boat side on and then stepped ashore herself to secure the stern. Acheson had the excited, guilty sense that he was witnessing something almost forbidden, and found himself simply unable to go indoors. Caterina lowered the hook of the little blue crane, to which Astrid attached a rope she pulled from under the covering. Then she too came ashore, and the two women hoisted the cargo, wrapped in canvas, on to the big metal table used for gutting fish on the quayside. They lowered the load, then Astrid pulled the covering away, revealing a swordfish, six feet long, its skin already blackening, its huge eyes red with fury and defeat.

When Acheson managed to stop staring at the vast fish, he realised that Astrid and Caterina were looking up at him. The women exchanged a glance, then Caterina giggled and gave a little wave, while Astrid saluted with a knife. Did she want him to go down and help to gut the thing? Unlikely. He shook his head and waved with what he hoped was a self-deprecating grin.

At least, thought Acheson, groggily standing in the shower long after his neighbours had breakfasted and set off to the nudist beach along the goat-path or somewhere equally demanding, at least now you have some idea of the identity of K. In his journal Wolf recorded a troubling attraction to a young local woman identified only as K. Somehow Acheson imagined Wolf as a man of about his age, which made what he described likely at the level of fantasy and wholly out of the question in practical terms. The local girls were mostly students back from Heraklion or Chania to help out their families during the season. They were not unsophisticated and they had their pick of the young local men. They also had brothers and fathers and uncles and entire regiments of female relatives keeping a discreet watch. If Wolf fancied himself as the grey-haired salt-caked Ulysses to K's Nausicaa, he was backing a loser. But as to the identity of K, internal evidence from the journal indicated that she might well be Katerina with a K rather than the C that Acheson instinctively used. After last night's adventure he was satisfied that Katerina was the girl in question.

Acheson went down to the restaurant for breakfast. He ordered bacon and eggs and coffee from the grave young waiter and re-read part of his translation:

In the middle of the night I heard a soft sound at the windows, which stood open in the heat. Then I saw a figure entering the room. By her faint outline I hoped without hope that it might be Katerina. But what could she be doing here? Without a word she came and lay down beside me on the bare sheet. I dared hardly breathe, until she turned and took me in her embrace.

Very literary, you dirty bastard. Acheson grinned to himself and closed the book, then jumped out of his skin.

'Why are you always working?' said Katerina. She put his breakfast things on the table. *Green eyes*, he thought, *or sea-cave blue, and round her neck a dolphin pendant. White t-shirt, the red shorts.* 'Your students have gone, Mr Acheson. If you do not relax now, when will you ever? You are not immortal. And also you should eat more good food. This –' she indicated the bacon – 'will turn you into a pig.'

The insult was unmistakeable but charming. 'Good advice,' he said, tongue-tied, the image of her sitting bare-legged in the boat suddenly before him again. She gave him the white, delighted smile she gave to everyone she spoke to, then disappeared into the kitchen. Ulysses had a point, Acheson thought a little later as he swam out from the more popular of the two beaches. Legendary island queens and enchantresses are one thing, complex and practised manipulators of men, but the true seductress is the pretty girl next door, the novice, sweet-natured but none the less pinned by desire and ready to act. He could not blame Wolf for his imaginings, unsubtle though they were.

Acheson rolled on to his back and floated, far out in the bay, over which the sun and the paling disc of the moon both now stood. The parched gold-brown cliffs studded with thyme and dwarf olive climbed fiercely into the waking glare of the sky. At last he turned over and swam steadily. He used the word 'Anna's' painted in blue on the white front wall of the house, as an aiming-point. As he drew nearer it occurred to him that he could easily approach the stone sea-god and get a proper look at it.

He paused in the water and looked out for it. Not for the first time a change of perspective gave the impression that the stone had moved further out into the water. The bay was bigger than it looked, of course. He swam on a little further through the water's alternating pulse of blood-heat and chill, sensing the white sea-floor dropping steadily away under him.

When his chest began to ache he paused and trod water. He was a long way out now. For a second or two he couldn't locate the sea-god, but then there it was, more or less where he expected it to be. He had veered off course, somehow, almost to the jaws of the bay. He should go ashore now. He was tired, and cramp could be dangerous with no other swimmers in the vicinity. It would be easy enough to go ashore at the nearer beach, the rocky one which lay next to Anna's house. The atmosphere of sombre Germanic sun-worship there tended to put him off, but he wouldn't have to stay.

He began to swim steadily back, intending to get a look at the sea-god in passing. Little by little – how small an impact his efforts were making now – the stone drew nearer, though its face, as he couldn't help thinking of it, naturally remained averted. Then, as if something had passed close to him in the water, he felt a sudden black adrenal burst of fear. He paused again, looking around and beneath him. Nothing there. What could there be? He had simply overset himself. But the mouth of the bay seemed much too big now, the water too deep, the sun too strong, and the visit to the sea-god was a project it would be wiser to complete another day. He changed course.

By the time he reached the beach where he had set out, he was exhausted.

Acheson awoke, drugged by heat, at 6pm, hearing the iron plates of the ferry ramp grinding on to the quay across the bay, and then the retaining weights kicked over by a crewman with a series of anvil-clangs that reverberated round the high-walled bay. It was important to see the ferry, Acheson found himself thinking, to be sure it came. He went on to the balcony. The passenger decks this evening were packed with people for whom this would be their only glimpse of the bay, its blue calm, its white-walled smile of invitation under the protection of the mountains. One time, next time, some of them would be thinking. Now Acheson wondered if he should leave in the morning. But there was no special reason to do so.

The restaurant was quiet that evening, so he was able to spread his papers over a table and work without distraction. When Katerina came to take his order, he said, 'That was a very big fish I saw you with.'

'I am sorry?'

'Early this morning. You and Astrid, with the swordfish.'

'Excuse me, Mr Acheson, but I do not know what you are saying.' She smiled, then nodded at the little glass pharos of raki on the table.

'I wasn't drunk,' he said, aware of the false, defensive note he struck.

'No, no.'

'I saw the pair of you landing a swordfish.' Katerina shook her head and laughed.

'The raki can bring powerful dreams. Very vivid.' She went on smiling. There was no criticism here, her expression suggested. The dreams were something well known, confusing until you recognised them. He looked round: the red boat rocked gently on its mooring nearby, its exuberant slash of

23

lipstick still in place. 'So, I am in your dreams?' she asked. 'With a swordfish? Best not tell my boyfriend in Chania, no? It will be our secret. Let me bring you a coffee. Megalo.' She disappeared into the kitchen.

Shaken, swallowing his embarrassment, Acheson accepted the coffee, paid for his meal and then took himself off to the bar by the ferry, where the perpetual hysteria of Greek pop music presented a suitable challenge against which to brace himself as he slogged on through Wolf's journal, sticking to Mythos beer.

It was late on in the holidays now, and most of the visitors seemed to be leaving tonight. Seeing these unknown twos and threes walk past, he felt what he almost never felt, the ache of loneliness, and as it blended with disorientation he feared for a moment or two that he would become unmoored. One thing he managed to insist on to himself: the physical weight and feel, the *reality* of the world in the swordfish episode – the steps under his feet, the muffled impact of the prow against the quay, the arthritic gasp of the crane against its housing as the women hoisted their catch aloft. He shook his head and turned to his only recourse in a time of crisis, writing things down.

Wolf was irredeemably high-minded. Everything the man encountered brought some literary reference to mind. If they had cut him open, index cards would have spilled out among the viscera. Meanwhile, on with the doom and the sex. Slightly to Acheson's surprise, Tennyson turned up among the references:

> 'As though to breathe were life.' Even the English bourgeois poet can understand the heroic impulse and how slow it is to die away. Even now I feel it, the desire to set out a final time, to escape the filthy enchantment of the bay. In Hans Castorp's vision in the snow he sees

the savage foundations on which the city is built, the
obscene sacrifice – what sacrifice, what maidens loth.
Time for me to take the ferry, or the red boat.

Das rote Boot. Acheson wrote the German phrase out
alongside his translation. Perhaps now that he had got the
sense of doom and the erotic reverie in place Wolf might be
moving on to consider suicide, or perhaps more likely a
mystical merger with the marine elements – oblivion
dignified with ritual. As a project it had its points, Acheson
thought. But what about the 'filthy enchantment'?

When he grew tired, he walked slowly back through the
blue dusk air, nodding at the waiters. They knew him by now
as a stayer-on. They sat on their stools by the tills of their
empty restaurants, watching the sea now that the ferry had
gone. As he skirted the beach he saw the red boat moving
swiftly outwards into the dark, a single imposing figure at the
tiller. *Watch out, swordfish,* he thought. That night he took a
sleeping pill.

He could not have said what time it was when he heard
the sound on the balcony. He lay, unable to move, as the slim
figure appeared in the open door and slipped on to the
mattress beside him, first taking his hand, then leaning over to
kiss him, her lips salty, her dark hair falling on his face and
chest. Still he lay paralysed, aroused and terrified in equal
measure.

When he awoke in the pre-dawn grey, he reached out
confusedly for his watch on the bedside table. His hand
brushed against something that seemed fleshy and muscular.
Still dream-heavy, he picked the round thing up and groped
for the lamp. In its light he held a thing like a monstrous
poached egg, its bloody gaze fading but still enraged, seeming
to pulse. He lunged for the window and hurled the eye of the

swordfish out into the bay and was scarcely able to reach the bathroom before he began to retch. When eventually he was able to stand upright, he looked in the mirror over the sink and saw a kiss of red lipstick planted over his heart.

Within an hour Acheson was showered and packed and ready to go. When he got off the ferry he would pick up a taxi over the mountains. But it was still too early. He put the journal back in the drawer and sat on the balcony. As dawn came, clouds were stacking up to southwards. For the first time, there was a breeze. The sea-god lay close in, its absent face impassive, the green chop breaking over its submerged shoulders. Acheson waited in an agony of impatience, until at 7am, when the breeze was freshening, he heard Anna and Astrid stirring below. He carried his case downstairs and tapped on the kitchen door. Astrid opened it and gestured for him to enter. A shutter banged somewhere upstairs and the rigging of the boats began an intermittent tapping. Astrid indicated that she must go and deal with the shutter.

'Please sit and join me,' said Anna. She was holding a cat, and dabbing at its gummy eye with cotton wool. To refuse hospitality would be rude in this domestic setting.

'I have had to change my plans.'

'Oh yes?' Anna said. She held up the cat to examine its eye. It wrestled a little in her hands, then she kissed the top of its head and released it. It took up a position on the draining board. 'How can I help you?'

'I will of course pay for the whole extra week, but it turns out I need to leave today.'

Anna smiled doubtfully and glanced towards the window.

'Is there something you do not like? Is the house, the room, not to your satisfaction?'

'No, no. All of that is fine. Perfect. But as you know, things come up.' He wondered why he was seeking to explain at all, never mind doing so with a lie.

'Things do come up,' she said, nodding. And now you wish to sail away like Ulysses to the ends of the earth and ocean.' Acheson smiled, at a loss to reply. The door behind him opened and closed.

'Mr Acheson wishes to leave us, Astrid,' Anna said.

'That is not possible,' said Astrid flatly. Acheson turned to look at her. She shrugged amiably and indicated the window. 'The storm.'

'What storm?' The glass rattled slightly in the frame, and Acheson could see darker swells building in the mouth of the bay.

'The ferry I am sorry will not come,' said Anna. She smiled apologetically. 'Astrid, make our guest some fresh coffee. Mavro and Megalo, I think.'

'Not until the storm blows itself out,' said Astrid. 'It is dangerous to sail in such weather.'

'The storm comes up from the North African coast at this time of year. It is called The Widow,' Anna went on, 'for those fishermen lost in it.'

'How long does it last? A day?' Acheson tried to make his tone ironical and unsurprised.

'There is no way of knowing. When the ferry comes, then it is over. Until then we eat what is in the larder,' she replied with a laugh.

'Sometimes it is a week,' Astrid added. She placed coffee in front of him. 'Like last year.' She smiled at the memory.

'When Herr Wolf was here,' Acheson said, wishing he hadn't.

'I am sorry. Who?' asked Anna.

'Nothing. Someone I know – he must have stayed in someone else's house.'

Acheson took his case back to his room and went out on to the balcony. The wind was gaining strength now, bumping the boats at their moorings, sending tall waves against the ferry-landing and the sea-god. Out to sea the sky was darkening and there was a trace of rain in the air. At a loss, he decided to go for a walk, but by the time he reached the foot of the steps the gusts were so strong that he must either return to the house or take shelter inside the café. The grave young waiter served him and stood beside the table, looking out through the closed door as though with satisfaction.

'All gone,' he said.

'I'm sorry?'

'All the strangers. The visitors. Excepting you.'

'All of them.'

'I think yes. Good timing.' He smiled at Acheson and raised his own cup, then inclined his head to indicate the bottle of Metaxa on the counter. Acheson shook his head and looked out as the storm arrived in full.

Eventually he struggled back up the steps in the torrential rain and then across the terrace. The bay was lost to sight. At Anna's the shutters were closed and the front door was locked. He felt his way round the house-end to the back. When he got inside there was no one to be seen. The office door was locked and the kitchen empty but for the cat now sitting on the table. He gave up and retreated to his room, feeling the gale leaning on the house as if to uproot it. At a loss, he unpacked his notes, then opened the drawer to take out Wolf's journal. It was nowhere to be found. After a time he sat listening to the storm.

He woke refreshed. The storm seemed to have died down, though the light was still muted. There was a knock at the door. It was Anna.

'We would like you to join us for dinner. Everywhere is closed still.'

'Is the storm over?'

'Yes, but there will be no ferry until tomorrow. It is too

late now. Please, we are ready. You must join us.'

The big kitchen table was set with candles and large platters of swordfish and octopus. Katerina smiled at him as he sat, then poured him a glass of bone-dry wine whose whiteness carried the faintest hint of green. At Astrid's urging he served himself food before finally Anna turned from the cooker with a flat pan full of dark fungus, the cat sitting watchfully on her shoulder. 'Quick. You must take it hot, then drink the wine. It is rare.'

'Here it grows only on the tiny islands,' Astrid said. 'I must go at night to collect it.' She gestured towards the window.

The wine was remarkable. It seemed to make the bones of his head sing as though with a far-off breeze. The tiny fungi – coiled, almost clenched like paws – had a rich, deep bitterness he half recognised. It demanded more wine, leading him back to the fungus in turn and on to the octopus in its ink and the melting flakes of swordfish that would have been enough in themselves. His hunger did not slacken any more than his thirst, and the three women watched approvingly as he ate. At last he was exhausted, watching Katerina pour the freezing raki into the decanter and then into his glass before raising it to his lips herself.

'Fit for a hero,' Anna said.

'Was Wolf a hero?' he asked.

'Wolf was no one,' said Anna. 'I mean that he was a creation. Or rather his book was, which I wrote to invite such a person as you.'

'Are you a hero, Mr Acheson?' asked Katerina, stroking his face. He was unable to reply.

'We must take what we can get,' said Astrid. Katerina tilted the tiny glass once more into his mouth.

He awoke unable to move, wrapped in canvas in the bottom of the boat, his head propped on a bench between Katerina's legs. She stroked his hair and whispered him to shush, though he could not have spoken. It was still dark but the moon was high and he could see the calm waters over which Astrid was rowing them. Anna was in the prow looking out. Now Astrid turned the boat slightly and he could see the raised head of the sea-god approaching steadily over the water. Beside him a bundle or a bag squirmed and mewled. That was the worst, perhaps because the cries had such domestic familiarity. The god itself was a terror he seemed to be witnessing almost indirectly. It had a face at last. Of course it did. Now, as the boat came close, and the sound of the oars ceased and Astrid and Anna manoeuvred him to the gunwale, his fear came in full, uncorrupted by habit or translation. In the white water the god had risen. Its tentacles beckoned. In its stone face, emerging from the water, its churning, many-tongued mouth lay open to receive him.

To See How Far It Is

'FOR GOD'S SAKE, SHUT up' said Mungo, pulling out into the thin early morning traffic. For a moment I thought he meant me. There was a song stuck in my head and my mouth that autumn, 'Dead Flowers' by the Stones, from *Sticky Fingers*, in particular the line about the girl who thinks she's the Queen of the Underground. But Jack was much worse, courtesy of a bag of yellow Dexedrine acquired from a passing Hell's Angel at a festival. Jack was lumbered with a verse from an old Cadillacs number, 'Speedoo': *'Well, they all call me Speedoo, but my real name is Mr Earl, / bop-bop-a-diddly / hoo hoo hoo / bop-bop-a-diddly,'* and he was still at it, over and over, as we drove out of town.

'Don't roll that in the car,' said Mungo.

'I'm not,' said Jack, continuing to do so. 'What you see me doing is practising. You won't complain when I offer you the perfect joint, will you?'

Mungo shook his head, resigned.

That October I remember as especially beautiful, on fire with red and gold along the Backs. The sun seemed to be inside the landscape somehow, a mellow valedictory warmth like a promise of who knew what? That morning, just after sunrise, a frosty fog blurred the edges of buildings and hung in the cobwebbed hedgerows. *Now*, I thought, *now it might happen*: since boyhood I had always wanted to be *inside* a story, and it seemed as if this could be it, the opening page of a narrative that had turned out to be true. I was so excited that

31

I didn't tell Jack: he would have messed around with the idea until it dissolved. Even before he took the speed he couldn't shut up.

He lit the joint.

'I told you not to do that,' said Mungo. 'Get busted, then what?'

'And that's why I'm not doing it.' Jack exhaled a rich cloud of grass smoke. Mungo wound the window down. 'Bosom pals, that's what we are, the three of us,' said Jack. Mungo looked at him without expression. It was sort of true, in the sense that we spent a lot of time together talking about books and listening to music and taking drugs.

We left the town, and the road rose towards the fiery wooded hills. Far off could be seen the incinerator tower of the hospital until the trees masked it.

'This is the place,' said Jack, and Mungo steered the car up a rutted chalk track through a wood of mature beeches. Once we were well out of sight of the road, he stopped.

'Now what?' he said.

'All experience is an arch wherethro' / gleams that untravelled world,' said Jack, climbing out and having a coughing fit.

'If you say so,' said Mungo.

'You're a theology student. You should know.'

'Then you're remarkably ill-informed. I have no expectations, metaphysically speaking.'

'Let's go,' said Jack, wittering that stupid song under his breath. *'Hoo hoo hoo.'*

We set off walking, me slightly to the rear, the junior third of the group, feeling lucky to be there at all, relishing the stillness and the frosty air.

The track went curving away uphill for a while, and the wood was quiet except for our boots among the leaves. Then the rise topped out and we began to descend among older, denser, knottier trees I didn't recognise. We crunched through a frozen stream that crossed the track, breath rising like fog. The sun fell, muted, through the branches. It did look very *narrative*, I thought. Something ought to happen, surely. Then I remembered why we were there. So did the others, it seemed.

'Shall we get on with it, gentlemen?' said Mungo. Jack took out his wallet and produced the three microdots.

'We don't have to do this,' I said. 'It's a nice day. We could just have a few spliffs and go for a walk.' Mungo gave a non-committal nod.

'Entirely up to you. Not compulsory.'

'One volunteer is worth ten pressed men,' said Jack, 'but of course, *"He who would valiant be, / Let him come hither,"'* Jack sang, in his smoke-damaged tenor. '*Hoo hoo hoo. Bop-bop-a-diddly. Hobgoblin nor foul fiend / Shall daunt his spirit.*'

'If you're sure,' I said. They reached out and took a dot each and swallowed them. After a second or two I followed suit. 'So now what?'

'His first avowed intent, / To be a pilgrim.'

'We walk and wait and see,' Mungo said, setting off downhill again.

'How will I know?'

'You just will. Believe me.'

I knew it would not be a good idea to be afraid. I looked sidelong at the others. They moved impassively through the chilly sunlight of the wood, like veterans, content to wait, with a better idea of what to expect. *Think of the story,* I thought, *think of the story.*

The track – a vehicle could scarcely have managed it by now – ended at a tall stone archway with padlocked wrought-iron gates. The padlock itself was rusty, and ragged willowherb had grown up among the bars. For no reason that I could see, we turned left and began to make our way along the high stone wall.

'Where are we going?' I asked.

'Does it matter?' said Mungo. 'It's a walk in the woods, that's all.' I'd always needed a reason to be doing something.

'Just follow the energy, man,' said Jack.

'Piss right off with that hippie shite,' said Mungo. Jack continued to burble bits of 'Speedoo' under his breath.

After a time we found a place where the wall had collapsed under a large fallen tree. We scrambled over the mossy, tumbled blocks into the denser woods of what seemed to be a neglected estate. This was trespassing, surely, but it felt like an invitation. We seemed to make no sound; nor could anything be heard in the woods that continued on the inner side of the wall. I wondered if I had gone deaf. Could that be one of the effects?

A faint path led downhill between silver birches and tall, rusty clumps of fern. A first flickering enrichment of colours in the visual periphery sent a little thrill down my spine. I turned to Mungo. He nodded.

'Yes, I can see it too. Here we go, I suppose. Jack! Hang on.'

'Where are we going?' I asked again.

'There and back to see how far it is,' said Jack. The red-gold wood glittered with frosty potential: *the story must be under way.* The voice of my thoughts echoing bonily in my head.

We saw the smoke first, a white curl rising out of the trees.

'I don't think we want to meet anyone, do we?' I said, but Jack had hurried on.

A little further on, round a bend in the path, we saw the place. Behind a stand of rowans crowded with crimson berries stood a two-storey cottage in grey stone, from whose roof the smoke rose. The building formed a right-angle on an overgrown yard with a much larger, apparently Victorian redbrick building with closed shutters. It looked as if the place had gone away somehow. I turned to say this to Mungo, but now I found he'd gone too.

For a moment I was lost among the melting colours in the frosty flagstoned yard. Had Jack and Mungo disappeared deliberately, for a laugh? I dreaded meeting anyone even more than being alone. Surely it would be obvious that we were off our heads? It could only mean trouble.

'There you are,' said a voice from behind me. I turned to see a pale, dark-haired girl in a long dress of scarlet velvety material. She was smiling. *Regal*, I thought boomily, *she looks regal*.

'I'm sorry.' I said. 'We didn't mean to... we just wandered in by accident. Having a walk and so on.' It sounded like nonsense.

I looked round. The others were still nowhere to be seen. Now I was observing as if from a distance.

'We were just wondering where you'd got to,' she said. 'It's getting on for dinner time.' Blues and crimsons flowed across her pale skin, then paused. For a moment she looked like a figure on a playing card, formal and arrested. 'Well, come on. What are you waiting for? It's chilly out here. You need warming up.'

I followed her round the corner of the cottage. A few hens picked at the gravel and a little way off on the edge of the trees stood some animal pens that stank of dung.

Time seemed to keep editing out bits of itself, because next we stood in a large kitchen with sacks of spuds stacked to one side of a long table, and bunches of herbs, and hams in muslin bags hanging on hooks from the blackened ceiling. There was an odd smell, both herby and metallic, that made me swallow and want to be outside again, but the heavy door was shut. A wood fire blazed in the vast hearth. Blackened pans crowded the hot range, and crows which I knew were not actually present walked about on the red hot surfaces.

Jack and Mungo were already seated in wooden armchairs before the blaze. They raised their glasses to me amiably as if pleasantly surprised to find me there, but they didn't speak and went back to staring into the fire. I found myself seated too, glass in hand, watching the flames where scarlet fish schooled and glinted. All this seemed enough to be going on with. There was something I ought be doing, or saying, but it stayed just out of reach, like the name of the story all this seemed to be.

I felt the girl's hand on my shoulder. 'Drink up,' she said, and I obeyed. The liquid had an odd, absent, slightly coppery taste, reminiscent of pomegranate, which I seemed to associate with underground. I drained the glass and looked up to find the girl standing before us, except that there were two of them now, hand in hand, and they were twins. The second had flaming red hair and wore a green dress, a heavy brocade where intricate spiral patterns pursued each other out of sight.

'What is this?' I asked. I looked round at Jack and Mungo but they seemed to be asleep now, their drained glasses tilted in their hands.

The dark girl spoke. 'This is our house. I'm Cissy and this is my sister, Kate. You are welcome to our house. We don't often get visitors here.'

'We didn't mean to intrude.'

'You were expected,' said Kate. Like her sister she seemed friendly but somehow official, too, as if following a series of procedures that need not concern me. She placed her wrist against the brows of Jack and Mungo in turn, then nodded to Cissy, who motioned for me to rise.

'You're welcome to dine with us, but there is a task we need you to perform.'

'A task? You mean work?' That sounded terribly difficult given the state I was in.

'A courtesy to us, the chatelaines of these woods,' said Kate, nodding slowly. 'Something we ask our guests to do before dinner.' The pans boiled and rattled and I realised that I was very hungry.

'The fire needs to be maintained,' Cissy went on. 'There will be no dinner otherwise. And we're busy here with our preparations and looking after your sleepy friends. Please go into the woods and gather fuel. Here.' She undid her belt and placed it in my hand. 'This is to bind the branches. Make sure you choose dry wood or it won't burn properly.'

'What about the others?'

'You can see they're resting. They must not be awakened yet.' Jack and Mungo stared blankly into the fire as if they were really elsewhere. 'You'll be helping us.' They were very beautiful, those girls, identical but different. Anyone would have done what they asked.

'And bring back some mushrooms and truffles,' said Kate. 'Use this purse. She detached a hide pouch from her belt and placed it in my hand. 'But make sure you don't eat anything before you return. We don't want any misfortune to befall you.' She placed her wrist against my brow, then nodded to her sister. 'He's fit to go.'

'But where should I look?' I asked.

'In the woods, of course,' they said as one.

'I'll be your humble logman,' I heard myself saying, but they had turned away to attend to the pans on the range.

I found myself walking among the trees with a sense of the house somewhere not far behind me. The dung-smell lingered, though there didn't seem to be any animals about. When I tried to remember how things had been before this day there was a dark emptiness and I became afraid. At that point I could have given up and sat under a tree with my head in my hands, but it seemed best to attempt the tasks I had been given: the darkness was probably a test I had to overcome, and anyway, I seemed to know that doing something was always better than nothing.

At first it was hard to tell the figure of things from the ground, and then trees, ferns, lichened green stones embedded among the seething red-gold leaves presented themselves in black outlines as if for inspection before resuming their place in the vast, evolving pattern. This too was beautiful, but I knew I must not look too long. People were waiting for their dinner.

Shaking my head, I began gathering firewood, hoping it was dry enough. Quite soon I had a sizeable bundle. I wrapped it in Cissy's belt and with a dizzying effort balanced it on my shoulder. Colours rained down from the canopy of branches in checkerboard designs, and I thought I would faint, but gradually my vision cleared a little and I remembered that my second task was to gather mushrooms, and that truffles had also been mentioned, whatever they were, outside a box of chocolates.

Sure enough I soon saw a clump of mushrooms thrusting its way through the fallen leaves at the foot of an ash-tree. I set down my burden and began to collect it. I knew nothing about fungi but was anxious to follow the girls' instructions. One or two looked safe; others gave out a black secretion and a vile smell; but who was I to know what was what? The girls could choose whatever they wanted. A third kind I thought might be fly agaric and these too I slipped into the pouch. I quickly filled the pouch and tied the drawstring to my belt.

But what about truffles?

A black pig appeared, nosing among the leaves as if it belonged there. It stopped, studied me for a few moments, and then went off again, occasionally glancing back. I dimly remembered reading something about pigs and truffles in France, and the word *Perigord* appeared in my head like a woodcut in a thought-balloon, the lettering wrapped in roots, with truffles nestling among the roots like little Scotch eggs, and a woodcut of a cheerful French pig reaching instructively towards the prize with its jaws open. The lines from 'Speedoo' drifted through my head like subtitles. I hurried on. The pig had found something under a tree and was trying to snout it up, but I reached in and plucked the dank little rough-skinned stinking growth away. The pig looked at me reproachfully and then set off again. By this means I gathered half a dozen of the dank, sweaty truffles, which would surely be enough.

I was about to pick up my bundle of firewood and return to the cottage when another plant caught my eye, a plain white star-shaped flower that looked like a snowdrop but remained upright on its stem. On impulse I went to pluck it. It resisted with a strength out of all proportion to its size, and in the end it took me both hands to drag it from the earth. At its root was a round black bulb the size of a small beetroot. This was not what I had been asked for. It had not been mentioned at all. I put it secretively in my pocket, looking nervously about me, although there was no reason to think I was observed, since as far as I knew everyone was back at the cottage awaiting my return. The pig was nowhere to be seen.

No sooner had I set out than there was a terrible noise, a tuneless roaring and squealing that seemed to want to turn into speech but could not. I felt myself turning blue with fear. I wanted to run but had no idea where to. Everything stopped to listen, then the noise sank away and the silence of the woods resumed. Where were the birds? Could they all have left for winter? Shouldn't there be the sound of a stream somewhere?

I shouldered my burden again and made my way back to the cottage. The hens scattered as I entered the yard, and there was a snorting noise from one of the pens. Leaving the firewood by the kitchen door I went over and looked into the pen. The black pig was rooting among a stack of turnips in a corner of his enclosure. He stopped eating and looked up at me and announced in his cracked pig-voice, *'Well, my real name is Speedoo but they all call me Mister Earl, / Well my real name is Speedo but they all call me Mister Earl / Bop-bop-a-diddly / Hoo hoo*

hoo/ Bop-bop-a-diddly', then turned glumly back to his turnips and continued crunching on them.

Again I wanted to run away but I knew I must look in the kitchen. I peered round the door. Cissy and Kate had their backs to me, busy at the vast table with I couldn't see what. Jack and Mungo were nowhere to be seen. The fire in the grate roared red and a second pig, this time headless, was turning on a spit, its fat fizzing and dripping into a long, blackened tray. I must have made a noise because the girls turned, butchers' knives in their crimson hands, their starched white aprons sodden with blood, and smiled at the sight of me.

'Just in time for dinner,' they said. Between them I saw a boar's head, its eyes still bright with terror, the long tongue flapping from its mouth as though the creature were trying to speak. Cissy smiled and brought her blade down and severed the tongue. The creature gave a great shapeless cry and as the light of horror faded in its eyes. Mungo's face passed across the pig's dead face and vanished.

'What have you done?' I said.

'What does it look like?' they asked in unison, wiping their cleavers on their aprons. Suddenly they were on either side of me.

'Bring in the firewood,' said Kate.

'Did you fetch the mushrooms?' asked Cissy. I handed over the wallet and brought in the wood, afraid to stay, afraid to run.

'Sit down now. You must be hungry,' Cissy smiled. Things faded again and I came round to find Kate putting a dish and a spoon before me. Strips of pork lay among the black juice of the mushrooms. The food stank of rot and earth and blood. 'Eat,' she said.

'You need building up,' Cissy said, placing her hand on my brow again.

'I don't think I'm hungry.'

'Can't let it go to waste,' Kate said, as if to a stubborn child.

They stood before me and joined hands. Their knives were somewhere out of sight now.

'Is there any salt?' I asked, and before they could reply I did as I knew I must do in the story. I took the black bulb of the white flower from my pocket and bit into it. The taste was earthy and bitter. I waited.

'Where is he?' screamed Kate. 'Where's the little runt? He's vanished!'

'He must have found the moly root in the woods, dammit,' said Cissy. They began to approach down either side of the table, knives in their hands. I slid underneath and then ran out of the door and leapt over the wall of the enclosure. The pig Jack opened his snout to sing again but I held it shut while the sisters ran past into the woods, roaring with fury, knives in hand.

All day they searched and called, coming and going, raging at me and each other. At last when it began to grow dark they returned and went into the cottage and shut the door. Crouching in the enclosure, I looked at Jack, who was reaching the end of the turnips.

'Can you come with me?' I asked. He shook his head sadly and turned back to eating. I slid out of the pen and away through the woods. I wandered for hours in the freezing dark, my teeth chattering and the fate of my friends playing over and over in my head, to the tune of 'Speedoo'. It was bitterly cold, the blue dark lit with a heavy frost. I thought I might never escape. But eventually I followed a stream downhill until as dawn came it ran beneath a high stone wall.

I climbed the wall and found myself among Nissen huts and outhouses and then at the rear of a large building which I recognised by the vast chimney of the incinerator. There I was found by a porter and fetched inside, after which things grow vague for a long time until I found myself in this room talking to you, Doctor, as I have done regularly ever since, while you sit at your desk and make the odd note, clearly not believing a word I say, even though – and I know it sounds incredible and mad – this is a true story despite being, in some respects, I admit, a bit weird.

Every time I ask about going home you change the subject. This morning I looked in the mirror – I don't like to do that too often, for some reason – and found my hair turned grey, as if years, decades, had slipped by in here. My hands shake and my words stumble and when there's bacon for breakfast I can't stop screaming.

So is this it? Am I to be penned in here like poor Jack pig with his turnips? I must have told you a thousand times: if you want to know the truth go and ask Cissy and Kate. They're only over the wall. They'll still be there. Or are you their sister too, Doctor? Are you the Queen of the Underground as well? *Bop-bop-a-diddly/ Hoo hoo hoo.*

The Good Stuff

WHEN SHE OPENED THE front door it seemed that Mrs Yorke had forgotten the appointment. She was tiny and grey. She had the faint stylised hesitation found among those who are never entirely sober.

'The manuscripts. We arranged to have a look at them, Mrs Yorke. James Fisher – from the Library?'

'Mr Fisher,' she said, as if only now seeing him. She led him into the hall; a dim space with an ancient hatstand, and in its mirror he caught a glimpse of her grey, anxious face. These things could be difficult: you didn't want to be negotiating with someone not up to it and always starting again. But it was part of his profession to be patient.

'I'll take you through,' she said, and he followed her down a passageway past the kitchen and out through an open door in to the garden. It was badly overgrown, the lawn knee-deep, too many trees, the shrubbery anarchic. Could the money have run out? Fisher wondered. It seemed unlikely. Though not a Big House of the pseudo-genteel kind, the place was substantial, a mid-Victorian rural residence in its own grounds, within reach of the railway, discreetly hemmed in these days by similar properties.

They passed through a stone archway and matters improved. There was a neat strawberry bed, and raspberry canes, an orchard and what seemed to be medlar trees, with a flagged path leading to a further substantial brick building overgrown with wisteria. Mrs Yorke produced a set of keys, opened the door and the handed the bunch to Fisher.

'Mr Fisher,' she said, summoning an effort of concentration, 'I find it – at the moment I find it – too painful to go over the papers myself. Left to myself, I would leave it all alone, but there are... necessities, of course. So I give you carte blanche with the papers. I wish you to catalogue the materials and give me, ah –'

'That would depend. It's not for me to say, I'm afraid.'

'Of course.' She made to go, then turned back, with an effort of attention. 'I have to warn you that I have no idea how long this will take or precisely what you will discover. I had no part in my husband's activities. I never interfered.' *How have you spent your life, then?* Fisher wondered. 'My husband was, however, clearly extremely... prolific,' she went on. 'There are, I know, a great many manuscripts, not to speak of... ah... voluminous correspondence.' She was walking a tightrope of elocution.

'Then perhaps I should begin and take a look.' She nodded, her duty done.

'I will ask the girl to bring you some tea.' Mrs Yorke looked at him carefully for a moment, then nodded and with a faint sad smile went slowly away. The faintest breeze would knock her over. Yet he could see she had been beautiful, with the pale, luminous skin and abundant auburn hair of one of the deadly Victorian naiads in a Waterhouse painting. Fisher wondered again what she did with her time, apart from drink.

As writers went, Edward Yorke had been markedly well-organised. The bookshelves were neatly maintained. Reference books. History. The occult. No fiction. A portrait by Augustus John confirmed the image of Yorke as a red-faced leonine clubman. Next to it, more surprisingly, hung a Sickert roofscape.

Fisher unlocked the interior door and found a small kitchen, bathroom and a bedroom. Then a further door to unlock, which opened on to a storeroom, the size of a double garage, with a final door providing, Fisher supposed, another exit from the grounds. Rather than windows there were skylights, their light muted by overhanging branches in full summer leaf. Narrow aisles ran between roof-high shelves of buff-coloured box files, meticulously maintained, with titles and dates marked in black ink. Yorke's workplace was in effect a separate, self-sufficient property. And the archival effort involved seemed too much for one man, let alone one who had always been absorbed in new projects.

Apart from filing, Edward Yorke seemed to do nothing but write. From the day he gave up his job at the bank in the City, he had given up the world in favour of language. No, Fisher corrected himself, in favour of *writing*, which was not the same thing. If Fisher had been in Yorke's place, he liked to think that language would have been the important thing, not worldly success. But as it was, lack of worldly success prevented Fisher, so he told himself, from testing his claims.

Yorke had been popular, enormously so – a little faded in the last few years as tastes inevitably shifted in the post-war period, but still a name familiar to a wide public, both those who visited libraries regularly and those who might occasionally happen on a book, or be told about one, or see books referred to in the newspaper. When un-bookish people thought of writers, Edward Yorke was an example of what they meant. A proper writer, with shelves of the stuff to his name, not a poet like Fisher.

Yorke's literary estate was not, of course, the sort of thing a university library should normally concern itself with, but Grindle, the Head of Acquisitions, was a visionary of sorts. He had made it known that since, sooner or later, most of the good stuff would be spoken for, they should look carefully at the less good stuff in the expectation that the evident decline in standards of taste would spread to the academy in due course. Then they would be ready to meet the demand. But where, Fisher wondered, did you draw the line? Grindle would no doubt rule on this when the time came. One thing was certain: if they didn't buy the manuscripts, the Americans would, and if there was one thing the Head of Acquisitions liked less than bad writing it was Americans.

Fisher left the dim space and returned to the study in time to hear a knock at the open door. A young woman stood there with a tray of tea-things. This must be 'the girl', though she did not look like a servant.

'You will be Mr Fisher,' she said, in a manner that seemed elusively mocking and inviting. 'Aren't you going to invite me in? I've brought some tea.' She took the tray to a low table near a settee and without being invited sat down and began to pour two cups. 'Don't let it get cold.'

Slightly dazed, Fisher did as he was bidden. 'I'm Caroline,' she said. 'I'm sort of a niece. I'm here, well, helping, I suppose. Not that there's much I can do. I suppose it's all right to smoke in here? It's such a bore having to go in the garden. The widow won't allow it in the house, of course. Liquid only in there, I'm afraid.'

Fisher found her an ashtray. Caroline waited for him to light her cigarette, then sat back and gazed at the ceiling as though it was his turn now. He could see a resemblance to her aunt, but the girl was jet-haired, more severe, with bold lipstick and dressed in a neat red suit, for town rather than the village.

'So what do you think?' she asked.

'I've only just arrived.'

'No, I mean the stuff, the books and stories. What do you think of it?'

'I don't have an opinion.'

'Oh, but you must. You don't like them, do you? You think they're ghastly trash, don't you?'

'As I say, Miss —'

'Call me Caroline. And you're Patrick.' How did she know this? 'Your secret's safe with me.' She looked at him steadily, then smiled and stubbed out her cigarette. 'Got to go. Lunch is cold, served at one o'clock, up at the house.'

'I shall be busy. I brought sandwiches.'

'Suit yourself, Mr Fisher. Patrick.' They rose, and off she went up the path, leaving him to gaze at the seams of her stockings. When she disappeared through the arch he took a notebook from his briefcase.

Caroline was right. Edward Yorke's writing was trash, supposing you compared it with Henry James, but of course most people didn't. Yorke had specialised in supernatural romances – devil-worship, demons, vampires and lurid though imprecise eroticism, interwoven with reactionary politics, whereby the threat to the order of things came either from the Communist east, or from the Jews, or preferably both. It was a mixture which seemed to speak to the grubby heart of England. Yorke's day was done, but there were plenty of readers who weren't bothered about that. Yorke might be dead, but he hadn't taken it lying down.

In one of the desk drawers Fisher was delighted to find Yorke's own catalogue of his work, a comprehensive-looking document dating from the autumn of the previous year. He had died in January and it had taken his widow six months to act. Sooner than some. Yorke's numbering system for the boxes should be easy to follow. Could Jane Yorke really not have known the state in which her husband had left his papers? Could there be a separation of realms as absolute as that would imply?

Fisher wanted to complete an initial survey as quickly as possible, checking the contents of the files against the catalogue. He carried them back to the desk one by one and went through them. To call Yorke organised was putting it mildly: for the novels there was a first draft in ink, second draft typed and revised by hand, final copy (never more than three stages of composition), galleys, final corrections, all signed and dated. There were eighty novels, written between 1910 and 1950. It was an epic of routine. And six hundred short stories. And journalism by the yard. No journals, apparently, which was odd, given the meticulous record-keeping. No wonder Yorke had died at his desk. And it was bound to be tosh, all of it, mediocrity and worse, on an industrial scale. But good reviews buttered no parsnips, Fisher reflected.

The following morning he went first to the library to give Grindle an initial report on the material. The older man was grudgingly admiring of Yorke's neat habits.

'It makes our life a lot easier,' he said. 'What about the widow?'

'She seems rather withdrawn and distracted. I wondered if she was drunk.' There was, he considered, no reason to mention Caroline.

'I meant: she hasn't changed her mind, then. They sometimes do when they see the undertaker coming up the path.' There was something cruel and pleased about Grindle.

'No, she just asked me to assess the material.'

'Don't mention money,' Grindle said, sharply.

'Of course not. I wouldn't. Anyway, I haven't finished yet.'

'How long do you need?'

'A week. Maybe a little less.'

Grindle sniffed. 'Yes, well, think on, Patrick. Off you go.' Grindle's all-purpose air of suspicion and disapproval never failed to work on Fisher. He went down the stairs itching with unidentified guilt.

He worked on through the week. Each day Mrs Yorke would answer the door and leave him to work. There was no sign of Caroline. Then, on Friday morning, the front door stood open and no one came when he rang the bell. He called out and then after a decent interval moved swiftly and anxiously through the house and out into the garden. Still no one appeared. He went through the arch to Yorke's study and let himself in.

He set to work, fetching and carrying and checking in more detail. It was extraordinary, he thought, like a Platonic idea of literary productiveness: these words, in this order, by the million, assembled in a vast (and speechless) chronology. The novels took up 200 boxes, the short stories another 100, the journalism 99. Look on my works, ye mighty, and stifle a yawn.

Yet, while according to Fisher's sampling the books themselves consistently failed to rise above potboiling tedium, to confirm this had its own fascination, and Fisher's skimming of chapters and pages provided a sort of entertainment as recurrent motifs appeared: cellars, creepered buildings, ashtrays with smoking cigarettes in empty rooms, silk negligees, ropes, fires, little men in Homburg hats, black candles with a poisonous light, floods, descending ceilings (see also rising floors), small exclusive restaurants, 'Je Reviens' and so on. What would Grindle instruct him to offer for the material? Suppose it had been Edgar Wallace, would that be comparable? No doubt Grindle would have his own arcane criteria. Widows and orphans beware.

When at last Fisher got to the end of his survey it was late afternoon, and once more baking hot. There was a peculiarity. Yorke's catalogue listed 399 items: Fisher had counted 400. He felt an intense weariness at the idea of counting again. Did it matter, one more or less? He wondered, then felt ashamed, as though someone might have overheard his thoughts. Either do a thing properly, or not at all, he could hear Grindle saying. He went back into the archive and did the count again. Twenty boxes to a shelf, four shelves to a stack, five stacks in all. 400, minus one. Yet when he did a survey of the identical buff boxes by eye, the eye told him it must be 400. It could not be otherwise. Boredom or afternoon sleepiness had made him miss something. He counted again. 400.

He wandered through the building, at a loss. For a time, with a slight feeling of guilt, he lay down on the bed but could not sleep. As he made to rise he saw a book on the bedside table. He picked it up. One of Yorke's. *Scarlet Midnight*. More rubbish. He went and splashed his face with water, then walked in the inner garden, helping himself to the strawberries. It was the hottest part of the day, towards four o'clock. He could knock off and go home but he didn't want to have to come back again, though the girl might have made the trip worthwhile if he'd seen a bit more of her. He glanced through the arch towards the house and caught a flicker of movement. Peering between the overcrowding trees he saw Caroline on the first-floor balcony. She was wearing a red swimming costume and a wide straw hat. She waved.

'Are you ready for a drink?' she called.

'That would be nice.'

'Stay where you are.' He made his way back into the dim study. In a minute or two Caroline arrived with a tray on which was a bottle of gin, glasses, a jug of ice and sliced lemons. Now she wore a red silk robe over her costume.

'It's about that time,' she said, pouring the drinks.

'Is it? When you mentioned a drink I thought you meant tea. I tend to avoid alcohol in daytime.'

'Quite the Puritan. Oh, well. We're here now. Cheers.' She lit a cigarette and crossed her legs, then sat back with her drink. 'So what have you discovered?'

'Actually, Caroline, I'm not really at liberty to say.' She snorted.

'Don't be pompous. Honestly!'

'It's a confidential matter between the university and Mrs Yorke.'

'Oh, she won't care.

'I rather think she might.'

'And she won't know.' She sighed and looked at him over the rim of her glass.

'How is she, actually? She didn't look very well.'

'Tragic widow. What do you expect? Old Yorke used to fuck anything that moved.' Caroline appeared quite shameless. 'It's OK, you know.'

'What is?'

'The good stuff.'

'You've lost me.'

'Don't be a tease, Patrick.' He shook his head. 'The good stuff? No? You haven't found it yet.'

'There's a great deal of material on the premises,' he said.

'So you haven't found it while you've been in there doing your sums?' She seemed oddly well informed. Presumably she'd been in nosing about, with or without the widow's consent.

'What am I meant to be looking for, exactly?'

'Oh, I think you'll recognise it.' *Nothing ventured,* he thought.

'Would you like to come for a drink later on, Caroline?'

'Patrick, I'd love to, but I have my duties here, seeing to Mrs Yorke.'

'Never mind. That's a funny way to talk about your aunt.'

'Isn't it? See you later, perhaps.'

When she left he found it impossible to continue work immediately. It was partly the strong gin and tonic, he told himself.

Grindle would be expecting him to report his findings first thing on Monday. If something was wrong, Grindle would spot it. He went to work again, taking down the boxes in batches of five, checking the contents against his own listing and Yorke's catalogue. The count was 400 but Yorke said 399, and yet there was no discrepancy between the contents listed in Yorke's catalogue and those in the files.

Which could not be the case. Not logically. Not rationally.

On the shelves there were clearly 400 files. He felt stupid and angry. He repeated the process. The result was the same. He was startled to discover it was past nine o'clock. The long day was finally dimming but the heat was unrelieved. He was too tired to continue or think clearly now. Time to go home. But there was a bed here, he thought. It might save time. He went into the kitchen and looked in the fridge. There was a pork pie and a bottle of champagne with a handwritten label: *Drink Me*. He ate the pie standing up, then opened the champagne – a consolation prize for his futile efforts. Carrying bottle and glass into the bedroom, he realised that he had brought nothing with him to read. It would be a bit desperate to start reading a volume of the dead man's OED now. *Scarlet Midnight* lay on the bedside table where he'd left it.

He poured himself a glass of champagne, sat down on the bed and opened the book. It was a cheap wartime edition, the paper already freckled and ancient-looking. He finished his glass and had another, then propped himself up on the pillows and began to read. He didn't recall this one, but Yorke's work was all much of a muchness.

In the event *Scarlet Midnight* was a rather different proposition from Yorke's other books. It was as though the author had suddenly discovered how to write. The material itself was much like the remainder of his work. It was a tale of the supernatural. It involved investigation among the arcane, the pursuit of the facts among the thickets of camouflage and deception, but while Yorke usually favoured a group of heroes – a professor, a nobleman and their young protégé – this was the story of a solitary, and, again unusually, written in the first person. The main character, Chadwick Boon, was a successful author, tired both of the superficiality of his success and, perhaps to a greater degree, of his wife. He had resolved to add depth, or zest, or interest, by replacing the wife.

To this end he followed a trail of clues from his own impressive library through private collections in France and Germany until at last, in a castle of the Teutonic Knights in the frozen Lithuanian marshes, he discovered what he was looking for, the darkly rumoured *Codex Revelatoris*. This was an apocryphal work contemporary with the Revelation of St John the Divine. It had many points of resemblance to the book with which the Bible closes, but there were equally significant differences. The Baltic peoples were among the last in Europe to Christianise, and a powerful strain of paganism, involving animism and fire-worship, persists in the iconography of those cultures to this day.

The *Codex Revelatoris* emphasised a strong feminine element in the habits of worship. In it the Scarlet Woman of St John the Divine – a monstrous meretrix often interpreted as the Roman Catholic Church – was replaced by the powerful erotic divinity, the She-Sun at Midnight: hence *Scarlet Midnight*. The Codex, so the novel proposed, contained rituals by which an arch-mage might summon the She-Sun in human form and, drawing upon her powers, rule the earth with her in erotic perpetuity. Chadwick Boon had come to consider himself such an arch-mage. By various sleights he abstracted the Codex from the chain library of the Teutonic Knights' lonely castle and made his way back to his home in the Thames Valley in order to conduct the ceremony of invocation.

For this purpose Boon would have to draw energy from his wife. She would serve as a portal through which the She-Sun might enter the mortal sphere. It was his wife's very lack of energy, her petit-bourgeois inhibition, her depression and enfeeblement and addiction to sherry, that Boon told himself had driven him to this point (via numerous unsatisfactory affairs undertaken in plain view of said wife).

The ritual might conceivably do away with her. But we must all make sacrifices in a greater cause. In the event, however, the procedure of inviting the She-Sun into the human world of Boon's study-library, did not prove fatal to Mrs Boon, but the effect on Chadwick Boon was altogether more grave, and frustratingly the novel reached its end with his cry for help *de profundis* as the She-Sun threatened to burn his soul entirely away.

Fisher had to admit it was a good yarn, or, as Caroline put it, good stuff. He would look it up in the files in the morning. Imagine if it were the missing 400th item – wouldn't that be amusing? It was past three o'clock in the morning and he was slightly drunk on champagne when he put out the light and went immediately to sleep. His dreams were complex and intense, highly coloured and wildly erotic. There was a castle, an escape, a flight and an abiding sense of doom, but as soon as his eyes opened the details fled.

He was startled to discover Caroline was sitting on the end of the bed. She seemed to be wearing his shirt.

'Finally,' she said. 'I was beginning to think you were dead. Old Yorke died in this bed, of course.' He fumbled with his watch on the bedside cabinet. Eight o'clock.

'Caroline, what are you doing here? '

'Ooh, dear, I can't possibly imagine.' She pulled back the covers and climbed in next to him.

'You can't do that.' He made to get up, but she was surprisingly strong.

'Do what? This? Or this? Try to be more specific.' It was daylight, he noticed, but it was entirely silent outside – no birdsong, no traffic.

'I have to go to the university,' he said.

'Oh, I don't think so. This little room is everywhere.'

'What if somebody comes?' he asked.

'Well, that's the idea,' said Caroline. 'Start counting backward from 400.'

Verney's Pit

SUMMER WAS ENDING, NOT yet, but at any moment. It was still hot, the sky a saturated mid-blue with a haze of chalk in it; but, as the poet has it, soon they would sense autumn like the opening of the door of a refrigerator far away. And their youth was ending too, more insidiously, in an accumulation of habits and obligations and a setting of limits to what might be done, even to what might be wished for; not yet, not quite yet, but would they even be able to tell when the boundary was crossed and the terms were fixed?

They had all arrived together a few years back as newly qualified teachers at the same school. The setting was dull and remote, a dormitory out in the furthest reaches of commuterland. The work was hard, demanding and continuous. They found themselves fiercely committed to it. It ate time whole, by the month, by the season, so it was hard to get away. Older friendships were difficult to sustain and they found themselves glad of each other's support. Now they were couples – Kate and Sandy, Ellie and Nick. And now a point was approaching when matters would change or become irrevocably fixed. Towards the end of this year's summer term each of them had been struck by the comment of a visiting speaker in Assembly that while she had loved her time teaching in Africa, there came a moment when she must decide whether to stay there and become an expatriate, or return to what was still just about home. Darkest Sussex offered more amenities than the Cameroon rain forest, but it exerted a powerful pull none the less. Happy those who give in, perhaps. And where was home? Did you travel from or towards it? But they did not really discuss the matter. It was at once too large and too oblique.

It was a Saturday near the end of the long summer holiday. Ellie and Nick had just returned from Crete; Kate and Sandy had stayed at home. Now time was running out. The sun shone. The heat lay heavily on the downland. Sandy and Nick had been playing cricket in the afternoon, after which there was a barbecue at the pavilion. As evening came on, it would turn into a party. But from the outset Ellie had been agitating to get away. There was a fair on the edge of the forest. They should go, obviously.

'It's just a few poky rides, Ellie,' said Nick. 'It'll be a rip-off. Everything here's laid on. It'll be crawling with kids over there.'

'I'm bored. I want to go,' she replied. 'It's nearly my birthday.'

'I've never heard that one before,' laughed Kate.

'Well, I'm just resourceful,' Ellie said. 'And it's true.'

'In three weeks,' said Nick.

'The fair won't be there in three weeks. They'll have waltzers at the fair.'

'Why don't we just bow to the inevitable?' said Sandy, and stood up. 'You don't mind driving, do you Kate?'

'Don't I? That's good of me.' She wondered why she and Sandy had to go at all, but she said nothing about it.

There were indeed a lot of kids about at the fair – restless, bored, continually circling the little showground and coming up with the same answer: that this was it and that was all there was to it. And an hour was enough to exhaust its interest for all of the group except Ellie. They'd done the waltzers, the Ghost Train and a Wall of Death that seemed so ancient it should be in black and white, not to mention illegal. They'd had burgers and candyfloss that they didn't really want. And now they were at the shooting gallery.

Nick had refused to pay. It was a waste of money and they should leave. To prevent the row that was clearly on its way, Sandy paid up. He won. The stallholder indicated a choice between a pomegranate and a ring.

'I want them. I want both,' said Ellie. She danced from foot to foot, her blonde curls bobbing in the soft light. Everyone loved her, whether they liked it or not. She could be fierce in a classroom, injecting jolts of Shakespeare into the bland pupils, but away from work she seemed at times much younger, and exasperatingly loveable. But stormy behind all that, and driven, no one knew quite why or where.

'The ring *and* the pomegranate? Both of them?' asked Sandy

'Yes.'

'You need to choose,' said Kate.

'Why do I need to choose?' asked Ellie. 'If I want both?'

'Because, Ellie, I've only won one of them,' said Sandy. He looked at Nick, who stood to one side, effortfully impassive. Trouble was on its way. Please let it wait until the evening was over. If there was a row it would somehow bring the new term all the closer.

'Well, win another one, then,' said Ellie. 'It's not that hard, is it?'

'Now you're being a minx,' said Kate.

'That's right, I am,' said Ellie. 'So, then, Sandy?'

The saturnine stallholder cocked the air-rifle with an air of immense but not unpleasurable weariness, earned through years of such exchanges with gorgios. He offered the weapon to Sandy.

'Mebbe best do as the lady says if you want to keep her, guvnor.'

'You think so?' said Sandy. 'She's not mine, actually.' He nodded in Nick's direction.

'Thought so. She looks a flighty sort to me.'

Ellie was delighted at this.

'I'm a respectable schoolmistress, I'll have you know.'

'Somebody's mistress, that's for sure,' said the man, with a long-tongued leer. He held up the ring and the pomegranate for further inspection. 'So, let's be having you, gentlemen. Or are both of you scared of a challenge?'

'Anyway,' said Sandy, 'it seems a bit early for pomegranates. Is that a new pomegranate or a very old one?'

The stallholder smiled again. 'What I can tell you, guvnor, is that like this unique ring, the pomegranate is part of our classic range. Shoot well and you can possess both and give them to this beautiful lady as a tribute.'

'Shameless,' said Kate, laughing.

'Everyone's got to make a living, Miss. What about you? See anything you fancy yourself?'

'Oh, I'll be sure to let you know,' she replied. The man nodded, appreciating the riposte. 'Sandy,' said Kate, 'just get on with it, will you?'

'Yes, Sandy,' said Ellie, 'get on with it.'

'Well, why not let Nick do the shooting? I mean, wouldn't that make more sense?' said Sandy. Kate glared at the heavens. Nick shook his head and moved further off.

'Nick?' Ellie snorted. 'He can't shoot straight. Can you, lovely? Doubt if he could even cock a gun.' Nick grinned dutifully and looked away into the thinning crowd.

Suddenly it was evening, the neon of the rides lipstick-bright and alluring, the competing music resolving to bass thud and shimmer. The heat of the day remained. Kate spotted a couple of girls from school looking their way.

'It's getting on,' she said. 'Perhaps we should make a move, then, if you're not –'

'Right,' said Sandy. 'One moment, ladies.' He handed over a pound, loaded a slug and took aim at the moving row of dented miniature Tiger tanks. One shot was enough. The stallholder handed over the ring and the pomegranate, and winked at Ellie. Sandy felt he should give the trophies to Nick to give to Ellie, but Ellie simply took them herself. Then, passing the pomegranate to Nick without speaking to him, she put the ring on her engagement finger and held up her hand for inspection. The ring was a cheap copper band with a flake of turquoise that must be paste.

'Could that be a hint?' said Kate. Ellie tossed her head, raising her hand further against the fairground lights.

'I've simply no idea what you mean,' said Ellie. 'Anyway, a girl's got to make her own opportunities these days. Right, now what? We should have another drink.' Ellie wanted to extend the evening. They all did. Autumn was coming, and the new term and all the rest of it. This evening, let it wait.

'Evening, Miss Johnson,' came a voice from a group of girls. 'Are you on the razzle, then?'

'Like you wouldn't believe, girls,' said Kate. 'And you lot should be getting off home now.' There were laughs and tolerant groans.

'If we're going for a drink, what about the Greenwood?' said Nick.

'It's boring there,' said Ellie, twirling about, the white skirt of her cotton dress luminous in the dusk. 'It's where the old blokes go, the dead people with their dominoes.'

'Can you stop doing that?' asked Nick.

'Doing what?'

'Dancing about. Showing off.'

'Oh God, Nicholas, I'm *enjoying* myself for once. Is that too much to ask?' As ever, Ellie's mood could reverse in a moment.

'All I'm saying is that the Greenwood's not full of sixth-formers. We can have a bit of privacy.' He offered Ellie the pomegranate in shy tribute. She shook her head and peered at the ring again.

' *"The grave's a fine and private place, / But none I think do there embrace"*,' she said. 'Anyway, yes, I suppose it'll do. If that's all there is.'

'I don't want a late night,' said Kate, as they got into her ancient 2CV.

'You're only young once,' said Ellie, getting into the front passenger seat.

'Remind me when that was. I must have missed it,' said Kate, her mind on work. 'Put your seatbelt on.'

'I hate it when autumn comes,' said Ellie. 'I want it just to be summer. Autumn makes me feel like dying.'

'I get that teaching fourth year maths,' said Kate, but Ellie wouldn't laugh.

They drove away from the fairground, past a paddock where two horses were tethered to railway sleepers, and soon the woods, oak, beech, ash, moved in on either side of the road, still green, but heavy with expectation. The moon hung massively over the trees. Below the high forest the harvest was in.

'What are you doing with the pomegranate, Nick?' Kate asked.

'Holding it for Ellie,' Nick muttered from the back.

'Perhaps it should be eaten.'

'Has anyone ever actually eaten a pomegranate?' asked Sandy. 'Can you really eat them? Aren't they all seeds?'

Nick leaned forward between the seats, the pomegranate held out before him. It glowed, the red and yellow of its rind merging in an autumnal flush. Kate noticed its chill, waxy scent. Nick began to recite:

'On plains where the naked girls awake,
When they harvest clover with their light brown arms
Roaming round the borders of their dreams – tell me,
    is it the mad pomegranate tree
Unsuspecting, that puts the lights in their verdant
    baskets
That floods their names with the singing of birds – tell me
Is it the mad pomegranate tree that combats the
    cloudy skies of the world?'

Ellie, who had fallen quiet, turned in her seat to stare at him. They held each other's gaze.

The lights of the pub came into view where the road curved downhill. Kate parked the car on the grass verge. They sat in silence for a few moments.

'Well, I think that's very romantic,' Kate said.

'It's by Elytis,' said Nick, 'the Cretan poet.'

'I know that,' said Ellie. She turned away, got out of the car and walked towards the pub.

'Well, I think it's lovely, anyway,' said Kate. 'But won't it be too dark to sit in the garden?'

'I'll talk to her,' said Nick. He followed Ellie, who had disappeared through the arch of laurel and jasmine. He was still holding the pomegranate.

'We'd better give them a few minutes,' said Kate. 'It might blow over.'

'This is a mess,' said Sandy. He reached for Kate's hand and kissed it.

'Someone will see,' said Kate. She smiled in the dim light inside the car.

'I don't see why we always have to be so respectable,' said Sandy.

'Because somebody has to. So behave yourself. And just now we have to keep an eye on those two.'

'What do you think will happen?' Sandy asked, after a while.

'Your guess is as good as mine. I think Nick's going to propose. Which in his mind means they stay here and buckle down and save up and get a house. And she wants to pack it in and go and teach English in Greece, and for him to go with her and not to worry about the future because now is now and later is later –'

'– and in the long run we're all dead. I can see the appeal.'

'Yes,' said Kate, 'but you wouldn't do it.'

'I might.'

'You bloody liar. No you wouldn't.'

'Yeah, you're right. It's you. You're holding me back.'

'Just you be grateful, then,' said Kate, and squeezed his hand.

'And what will Ellie say if he does propose?'

'God knows. And in the meantime we'd better go and see what's happened to them. Triage may be required.'

The bar was empty but for a couple of the legendary old men wordlessly laying down their dominoes. The pieces tapped like bones. Sandy bought drinks and followed Kate out into the dim garden under the oaks and limes. A single lamp hung from a trellis like an act of homage to the moon. Ellie and Nick were nowhere to be seen, but Ellie's bag stood on a table by the back gate beside a couple of empty wine glasses. The pomegranate had been cut in half and one half scooped out. A few seeds lay on the table.

'Has she gone to the loo?' asked Sandy. Kate shook her head impatiently.

'Ellie may be scatter-brained but she'd hardly leave her bag. And where's Nick?'

'Maybe they set off walking back.'

'The bag, Sandy. Anyway, it's miles. And her sandals have heels. She couldn't get far in those.'

The wicket gate at the back of the garden stood open. They looked at each other.

'Maybe we should leave them to it,' said Sandy. 'You know, a lovers' quarrel, and then they make up.'

'Anyone might see though,' said Kate.

'Well, I don't want to see. It would remind me of what I'm missing what with all this being a grown-up business. I think we should wait. They're obviously coming back. I mean, as you patiently pointed out, there's her handbag.' Sandy sipped his pint, unconvinced by his own argument. Kate stood with her arms folded, looking at the gate.

After a minute Sandy said, 'Yeah, OK. Better have a look, just in case.' Kate took the handbag. They went through the gate into the wood, joining a bridle path between banks of ferns. There was moonlight enough to find the way.

'What's down here?' said Kate.

'Not sure. I think it probably leads to Verney's.'

'What's that?'

Sandy stopped to light a cigarette.

'Verney's Pit. It was a quarry, ages ago.'

'I don't like the sound of that.'

'There's a pool there now. These old workings tend to flood.'

'Why didn't you say something?' hissed Kate. 'You should have prevented them.'

'Eh? How could I tell where they were going?'

'Yes, well, anyway, better get a move on.'

'Did she tell you something?' Sandy asked.

'She didn't have to.'

'I mean, they're just having a row. They're not daft, are they?'

Heat stood among the trees. The pair went on in silence for a while. The path curved gently downhill. At last they came to a wire fence that had been flattened by people climbing over it, beyond which stood a faded sign: DANGER. NO SWIMMING.

'I think this is it,' said Sandy. Beyond the fence they passed through a belt of birches and hawthorns before coming out at the water's edge. The moon seemed larger than ever. In the flooded quarry, small grassy islands where birches had taken root went stepping off into the deepening blue distance, making it hard to judge the extent of the unmoving water.

'There,' said Kate. 'That's them.'

Off to the left two figures had emerged from the trees.

'Ellie!' Kate called. Ellie took no notice. She was pointing angrily at Nick.

As Kate and Sandy drew near, Ellie yelled: 'You're just fucking dead already, Nick. There's – there's – bloody nothing in you but dust and fear. I don't know why I ever had any hopes of you. You start quoting poems like you care about them, but you're just a straw man.' Her mouth was stained with pomegranate juice and sticky with seeds. Juice had soaked into the neckline of her dress.

Against her fury Nick was saying, in a quiet monotone: 'I just don't think it's a good idea just to go off into the wide blue yonder. Not now.'

'Then when, for God's sake, when? Time is passing!'

'In a while, perhaps. We'll have to see.'

'You mean you want to get me tied down here keeping house and minding your kids.'

'Don't you like children?'

'Whether I do or I don't is irrelevant, you fucking moron!'

'I may be a moron, Ellie, but you need to think, because time is passing.'

'You can't say that! I've just told you that!'

'Perhaps you need to calm down,' said Kate.

'Or you need to piss off and mind your own business,' snapped Ellie. 'I know whose side you're taking, you boring cow. You're another one the same as Nick. You're all the same. You're bloody finished. I'm going and you can't stop me.'

'Please don't,' said Nick, dogged as ever. 'Ellie, I've said I want to marry you.'

'To stop me leaving. What reason is that?'

'Let's go somewhere and talk about it,' said Kate.

Ellie looked at them in turn. Her eyes were large and full of tears. She shook her head, turned away and stepped into the water, pulling her dress over her head and throwing it aside.

'Just go away and let me be,' she said, and slid into the lake, swimming firmly away.

'Oh, Jesus,' said Sandy. 'She must be crazy. God knows what there is in there.'

'Ellie, come out!' Kate yelled. 'It's dangerous!'

Ellie paused in the water, turned and looked expressionlessly back for a few moments, then swam on.

Nick pulled off his shirt and jeans and ran in after her.

'Not him as well!' said Kate. 'We need to get help.'

'There's no time,' said Sandy. Ellie had disappeared between two of the grassy islets now. Nick hauled himself half on to one of the grassy humps, and yelled after her, then he slid back into the water and he too moved out of sight.

'I'll go in,' said Sandy.

'No —'

'Listen. Go back to the pub and get help. Go. I'll find them. But get help.'

Kate ran back along the path, hearing the splash as Sandy went in.

The woods were silent as Kate hurried along. She wondered if she was lost. Where the path turned she came to a startled halt. The stallholder from the shooting gallery was slowly approaching on horseback, with a second horse following.

'I need to get past,' Kate said. 'There's been an accident.' The man shook his head as if dismissing this claim. He dismounted. 'Didn't you hear?' Kate said, more loudly. 'Let me past.'

'Nothing you can do, lady. Not now,' he said.

'Don't be ridiculous!' She found she didn't want to push past him. His horse whickered in the shadow and began to graze. 'What do you mean?'

'I dunno about what it means,' the man said, stroking the horse's long chestnut neck. 'I'm just saying it's what happens.'

'Are you crazy?'

'More than likely.'

'They need help,' Kate said. 'You could go and help while I ring.'

'Who you going to ring that can help them now?'

I cannot really be standing here discussing this, she thought. She breathed in the warm, meaty smell of the horses, and of the man scented with tobacco and spice. It was like the dream in which the first intention is never fulfilled, and the true end quietly takes its place instead.

'Let's go and see, shall we?' the man said, easily, reasonably. 'Or you could take the other horse and we could be off and away. Wouldn't that be dandy? Off she rode with the dark-eyed gipsy? Seeing you can't help your friends. You want to see places, I can show you some. Come on, girl. Why not?'

'You are mad.'

'She ate it, didn't she?' said the man. 'She ate the pomegranate. I knew she would. She was dancing for it next to my stall. She knew what she wanted, that girl, and for sure it wasn't anywhere here. Wasn't anywhere that anyone can actually go to. She knew that.'

He's right, thought Kate. She turned back along the path, the man and his horses following. In her mind's eye Ellie was dancing, her mouth sticky with pomegranate seeds, her white dress plunged in red and russet. After a time she came to the water's edge. Sandy was sitting with his head in his hands.

'I got lost,' Kate said. 'I'm sorry.'

'What? Too late anyway. I couldn't find them. They were just nowhere,' he replied, without looking up.

Kate turned to the horseman, but he was no longer to be seen.

The next day, a Sunday, the weather thickened and hinted at storms. Verney's pit was searched by divers who confirmed that it was full of dangerous submerged obstructions – old machinery and fallen trees – and that there were deeper areas. But they found no one. Such places, everybody said – the police and the coroner and the headmaster and the older members of staff – prefer to keep their secrets. The tragedy, they went on, at the inquest and in Assembly, must serve as a warning to others to steer clear of such places for fear such a thing might happen again.

For no reason they could name, Kate and Sandy drifted apart. After a few months Sandy took a job in London. Kate stayed and was promoted. Headteacher by forty, she was told, if she played her cards right. She bought a house. It was all as normal as could be.

Years slipped past. When she noticed, towards the end of one summer holiday, that the fair was returning to the forest, she had no intention of going, but she found herself walking among the stalls and rides, through crowds of different kids with the same ancient restlessness. She realised she was looking for the shooting gallery. There it stood, on the edge of things. An old man was running it now. No sign of the horseman. She could hardly ask.

She paid, took the air-rifle and with the final slug hit the battered tank. 'What will it be,' the old man asked sleepily, 'the ring or the pomegranate, lady?'

She made her choice but did no dancing, then drove to the Greenwood and walked through the woods. The fence had been repaired and the sign repainted, but she got over easily enough. On the shore she sat on a stone in the moonlight and cut the pomegranate in half. It looked impossible to eat, too full of seeds, but then came the smoky bitter-sweet autumnal taste in her mouth, like a promise of a desire no one could entertain, in a place where no one could go. It was irresistible.

Change for Low Rixham

IN THAT UNEASY, BEAUTIFUL, far-off summer near the end of an age, the ruined man was glad to have the compartment to himself.

He lay in shallow, dry, restless sleep, waking intermittently to see the stave of telegraph wires rising and falling at the window. Once, rain lashed against the glass. He saw a rainbow falling into the woods, and later, he looked out to find the sky clear and the daylight moon receding into the intense late summer blue. Each time he slept, these new sights figured in his disordered dreams of flight and pursuit.

Noon came and went, and the train crossed rivers and little roads and skirted towns and villages, meres and ragged, nibbled commons. Chalk hills rose up, carved with a white horse. They shrank away again, and had the traveller been awake he might have seen the sea for a moment, a silver-blue thread wavering at the limit of vision. But he was tired, and worse than tired: he was ruined. To sleep was his best hope for the moment.

When he arrived at his uncle's house he would have to face not only the sorrow and pity of the kind old man, but also himself. He had fallen into error and made a fashion of it: trained for the law, like his uncle and all the male line of the Carews, he had wanted to turn poet and in order to do so had let himself be introduced, a little late in the day, to decadence, to the scented chambers of the Jade Dragon and the sweet sickness of the pipe, and the pipe had consumed him – body, mind, earthly substance and prospects, almost his spirit too. At last his friends had come and sought him out and put him on the train: his only hope of restoration, they believed, was a prolonged period of rural retirement and reflection, far from the capital and the lure of the Jade Dragon. Therefore, Carew was en route to the house of his Uncle Edward, remote as you please, where the old man busied himself among books and natural history, and where the staff – a housekeeper and a coachman-gardener – were waiting to receive the young man they remembered in the promise of his boyhood. In such a setting, if anywhere, there would be hope for him still.

After a time sleep deserted him and he tried to give his attention to a book, but his attention flitted restlessly between the page and the passing scene. He rose and went out into the corridor and along to the carriage-end. The other compartments had emptied along the way. He picked up a discarded newspaper and took it back to his seat and made himself read the leading article, which concerned German naval expansion and the need to match it. *War-sickness*, he thought. They have it, the editors, like the industrialists and bankers and politicians: it is a disease as all-consuming as my own. His eyes pricked with tears as he looked out on to the heavy gold fields of high summer, fringed with dark woods. A scarecrow looked back at the train, his spread arms seeming both to commend this English scene and to express resignation to what fate would bring.

Carew emerged from this passage of sorrow with a little flicker of horror. There it was, in the pit of his stomach and the base of his skull, the beginnings of a craving, like a voice so far off as yet to be inaudible, yet coming, coming, as certain as midnight. His friends had searched him at the station, but in the bottom lining of his Gladstone bag he had managed to secrete a little of the drug. *Which of course I will not take,* he had told himself. *It is only for the gravest emergency, and where I am bound there can be no emergencies, not at Uncle Edward's house.*

He read on, through the letters, the news from the criminal courts and the foreign correspondents and the gazetteer, then went back to his book and strove to control himself.

In the late afternoon, with the air heavy with scents and the promise of a thunderstorm, the train ran into a heavily wooded cutting and began to slow. A neat station in yellow brick appeared, its awnings hung with tubs of flowers. There was a call: 'Change for Low Rixham. This train proceeds to Market Henry. Change for Low Rixham.'

Startled, Carew pulled his bag down from the luggage rack and made his way on to the platform. He had not known that he would have to change. In former times the train had gone directly to the halt nearest Uncle Edward's house. Now, as he looked around for the porter, the whistle blew and with a jolt of its couplings the train drew slowly away, swallowing the bridge with a gout of smoke and steam. Sparks flew upward against the intense blue: the traveller dwelt on this for a moment, half-remembering.

Through the thinning cloud the stationmaster appeared, a broad, sombre figure in a moleskin waistcoat, with his peaked cap pulled down over his brow, motionless until with a nod he greeted Carew.

'When is the connection for Low Rixham to arrive?' Carew asked, uncomfortable in the gathering grey heat. There was no one else about. The man came forward, heavy-set, too big almost for his uniform, studying him carefully.

'Low Rixham you're wanting, is it, sir? I see.' The man stroked his moustache carefully and looked up and down the track.

'Is there a problem?'

'A problem. In a manner of speaking, I think there is.'

'Is the train late?'

'Not precisely, sir.'

'Are you making fun of me?'

'By no means, sir. Perhaps you would care to join me in the office? It's cooler there and I can offer you a drink. We shall have to cross to the other side.' Carew, baffled, felt powerless to do anything but accept the invitation. He could hardly expect the man to produce a train from under his waistcoat. He followed the stationmaster over a stone footbridge and down the platform to an open door next to the arch of the station's exit. Inside it was whitewashed coolness, bare boards, an empty highly polished grate, a couple of chairs, a desk and telegraph equipment.

'Have a seat, sir. Will you take a glass of lemonade?'

'That would be kind.'

The man poured two glasses and sat at his desk, still giving Carew his considering gaze.

'You were going to explain the delay – or whatever it is,' said Carew.

'I shall try, but first may I know your name?'

'Is that material?' Carew said, with an irritable laugh. The stationmaster nodded, half-apologetically.

'Otherwise I assure you I should not ask.'

'Very well. My name is Miles Carew.'

'Then welcome, Mr Carew.'

'I had not intended staying.'

'Nevertheless.'

'What on earth is the matter, man?' Carew considered finding somewhere to administer a dose. But he would not do that, would he? The telegraph chattered and the stationmaster rose to attend to it. There was a faint, far-off rumble, as though there were thunder underground. The man turned back to address him.

'Your train will arrive to time, in an hour, sir.'

'Then let me detain you no longer. I shall go to the waiting-room.'

'When the train arrives,' the man continued, as though Carew had not spoken, 'it will need to take on water, and this will occupy several minutes.'

'I suppose I'm not in a hurry, as long as I reach my destination. Thank you for the lemonade. My compliments to your wife.' The man smiled.

'I have no wife, sir. No wife or child. This place is what I have to hold.'

'That seems a curious way of putting it.'

'It is my duty, sir.'

'I would not make light of that. I admire those who know where their obligations lie.'

'When the train is halted here for water, that is where the problem arises.'

'What is the problem?'

'It is the other train.' Carew stared at him. The man looked back, unblinking.

'You mean a collision? But how could you know that? And surely – surely there is time to prevent it.

'Not a collision, no, sir.'

'In God's name, man, spit it out.'

The stationmaster's face darkened, but his sombre composure remained undisturbed.

'It is something you will need to see for yourself. It is not something that can be described.'

'I think I will continue by carriage. Please summon a driver.'

The stationmaster shook his head.

'No one will come, sir.' Carew knew instantly that this was true.

'Are you threatening me?'

'I would not threaten you, sir. Rather I must call upon your help.'

'How am I to help you?'

'When the time comes, you must help me to hold the bridge until your train has taken on water. Then you may depart.'

'But who could wish to – to take the bridge?'

'You will see that when the other train arrives.' The stationmaster turned away and unlocked a tall cupboard.

'And who else is here to help mount the defence?'

'The boy and Jacob are in the signal box. When the time comes they will protect the far bridge. We shall take care of this one.'

By rights the man should have been an evident lunatic, but his authority was such that Carew felt compelled to believe him in every particular, especially when the stationmaster took two Lee-Enfield rifles and a Webley revolver from a rack of weapons in the cupboard and laid them on the table before Carew.

'You know how to make use of these, I think, sir.' He took out boxes of ammunition, selected weapons for himself and secured the cupboard again.

'It's true I did a little rough shooting with my uncle,' said Carew. 'But that was years ago. How could you know that?'

'Trust the eye and the hand, sir.' They finished their drinks and went out on to the platform. At the far end two figures waved from the parapet of an iron footbridge. The stationmaster raised his rifle in acknowledgement. 'We shall wait on the bridge. Your train will arrive at the platform opposite where you came in. It will take on water. The other train will arrive from the north. Now we must wait.'

They stood at the stone parapet in the thick heat; the air seemed full of sour electricity. The birds had stopped singing. Thunder rolled again beneath the horizon. Carew found himself islanded in the slow present: here, this place, and the stationmaster standing motionless beside him, and the expected arrival of the other train: these seemed to be the sum of things. He was very afraid; it was as if he had never been otherwise than this, afraid and waiting.

The signal above them changed and in a minute or two his connecting train appeared, slowing on the curve as it emerged from the tunnel. It was a small local train, a cheerful stocky engine with three carriages, its livery a rich green. Soon it slid beneath the bridge and halted. No one got on or off. For the first time Carew registered that he was the only traveller on the station and that there were no signs indicating the place.

The driver's mate got down and hauling on the chain swung the tall trunk of the hose into position. He waved to the stationmaster, looked up and down the line and then waited on the steps of the footplate.

The signal shifted again. Now a train appeared from the other direction, emerging from the steep wooded cutting and sliding silently to rest at the platform. It was altogether bigger, a black engine, with half a dozen black and crimson carriages. In all of them the blinds were down. The stationmaster worked the bolt of his rifle. Carew anxiously followed suit. The two trains stood adjacent: Carew could hear water plunging into the thirsty tank of the local, but this seemed only to emphasise the silence of the more recent arrival. The sky, flickering with silent lightning, seemed yellow-green.

'Steady,' said the stationmaster.

An age went by, during which Carew thought he must faint from the thundery heat. Then came a single horn-blast and the carriage-doors were flung open. Instantly, innumerable scurrying black-clad figures crowded on to the platform, howling with vile, liquid voices, running towards the bridges at either end. Carew could neither count them nor make them out clearly.

'Take aim and wait now,' said the stationmaster. The worst thing, Carew thought, was the anonymity. The assailants' faces were completely masked with hoods and scarves, he now saw, and they all seemed to be wearing academic gowns, which flew out behind them. They were armed with swords and axes and what seemed to be rakes of some kind. Now, as they neared the base of the bridge, the stationmaster spoke.

'Fire at will.'

It was a slaughter, the first half-dozen hit, howling and falling in the confined space of the platform, and the half-dozen after that following and falling in turn, the next line vaulting over the dead. The two men's rifles emptied, and they could hear the fire laid down by Jacob and the boy on the far bridge.

'Reload for us,' the stationmaster commanded, aiming his pistol into the crowd approaching the foot of the steps. 'Quick but steady.' Carew fumbled for a moment but managed his task. He rose again, handing a weapon to his companion and seeing the black-gowned host beginning to mount the lower steps. Again the two men fired, again Carew reloaded. And again. On the other platform the driver's mate was wrestling to get the hose clear of the tank.

'What is it they want?' Carew shouted.

'Is that not obvious, sir?' said the stationmaster. 'It is you they want. They have come for you.' Carew was sick with horror.

'This is the last of our ammunition.'

'When I tell you, sir, you must run for the train. Do not stop or look back.' They emptied their weapons into the crowd, but one figure was unhit and came skimming up the stairs, dagger in gloved hand. As it reached for Carew, the stationmaster seized it round the neck and plunged a knife of his own into the thing's chest. It writhed and grew still, and everything seemed arrested and waiting in that moment. The host on the steps had paused. Silence had fallen at the far bridge.

'I will show you what you are fleeing from,' said the stationmaster and tore away the mask from the corpse. The head was white and bald, and eyeless and noseless, its only feature a wide red mouth from which blood now trickled. 'Now go!'

As Carew reached the steps, he disobeyed instructions and looked back. The stationmaster faced the silent crowd and gave a great cry. He seemed to grow in stature. As he did so, two smoky, flaming wings appeared on his back. For a moment the attackers hung back, then they surged upwards and the winged figure laid about him before flinging himself into the baying host, wielding the dagger.

Carew leapt down on to the platform. The train was already pulling away as he wrestled open the door of the nearest carriage. They gathered speed. He found a compartment and looked back along the platform. There were figures in pursuit but falling back. He sat down and closed his eyes for a moment. When he opened them again, one of the black-cloaked creatures was clamped to the window by its red, sucking mouth, its face like a white leech against the glass, feeling to get in. Carew rose in horror and at that moment the creature was swept away when it struck the narrow mouth of the tunnel. Carew sat down, exhausted, while the train ran on into the darkness. Once again he closed his eyes.

When he awoke, his first thought was that he had left his bag behind in the stationmaster's office and with it the little supply of the drug he was not intending to use. He sat restless and exhausted, the empty rifle propped on the seat beside him. He found it hard to remember clearly the sequence of recent events. He had not taken in the name of the station. His mind could not settle to making sense of the last hours, and he had a terrible thirst. Again he half-dozed: the stationmaster's burning wings unfolded in his mind's eye, and he heard again the words: *It is you they have come for.*

When next he awoke, the thirst was torment. It felt as if time itself had stopped. It took him a little while to realise that the compartment was in darkness and that the train was moving very slowly, as though through a tunnel. He looked around and saw nothing, but heard a click, and then the door of the compartment sliding slowly open. *It is you they have come for.*

II

What She Wanted

MICK REVERSED STEVE'S VAN to the edge of the dunes. They got out and stood uncertainly. 'It wasn't like this when I came before,' said Mick. The temporary road of rubber and steel mesh had been forced right over on to the mudflats when last night's tide breached the landspit. Torn and buckled sections lay as if they had always been there. It was hard now even to make out the course of the original road.

The wind was strengthening. Faintly, a mile or so further on, they saw the lifeboatmen's cottages, and the black and white lighthouse beyond. The tide was on the turn. On the landward side of the curving spit, the flats extended back upriver, stubbly with weed and shoals of stone. The pipework of the gas terminal glinted against a slate sky.

Steve struggled to light a cigarette using his jacket as a windbreak. After a minute he gave up. 'So are we staying or going or what?' he said. He looked like shit. He looked old. His long grey hair was ridiculous. *I can't look as bad as that, surely*, Mick thought. He got the rucksack out of the footwell and put it on. The weight surprised him.

'Well, we're nearly there now,' he said. 'You said you wanted to. If you remember.' Steve shrugged.

A hundred yards on, the old road re-emerged underfoot and then ran between head-high banks of furze.

'Getting late,' Steve said, dawdling.

'We'll have been and got it over with, won't we?'

'We've been before. According to you.'

'How much did you have last night?' Mick asked.

'Fuck knows. A lot. Sorry, it's just –'

'I know.' Mick shook his head.

'I'm trying to remember if we ever came here, yeah?'

'You and Jules.'

'You'd think I'd remember.'

'Been a long time.'

'We're too old for this. Poncing about out here.' Steve had stopped and was looking around. 'Where is it you mean exactly?'

'At the end. Beyond the lighthouse. Where you said she said.' Mick spoke over his shoulder.

'It might not be there any more.'

'I did a recce, remember.'

'That was in spring. A lot could have happened.'

'A fort doesn't wash away.'

'Yeah?' said Steve. 'Neither does a road.' They reached the houses, a dozen of them, boxy, roughcast, an outpost. A couple of marooned cars waited where the road ended and the unmanned lighthouse stood. As a child Mick had wanted to live here with the lifeboatmen.

A woman glanced at them as she took washing from a line. They felt her gaze following them beyond the houses and past the lighthouse.

'I don't think Jules would have liked it,' said Steve. Mick laughed.

'But that was back then. What choice did she have? She went where you went. That was what girls did, remember?'

'It wasn't like that, really, man,' Steve suggested. 'Not as bad as that. I mean.'

'It was just that no one was noticing. The backward look is not very pretty,' said Mick, adopting the voice of an aged academic. 'Posterity, ladies and gentlemen, is a cruel mistress.'

'Eh? Fook off. She could have said she didn't like it.

Anyway, I don't think we ever did come here, not together.'

'You would have been off your head. It was a long time ago.'

'Everything's a long time ago now,' said Steve. They climbed a low hill, an impacted dune, overgrown with hawthorn and elder and brambles and criss-crossed by narrow foot-worn tracks that sank into the vegetation and were soon roofed in with green. Among the wild growth there were blockhouses half-submerged in the earth, and turntables for the naval battery. 'Fort' was a bit flattering for what this had been.

Even here litter was snagged on branches and thorns. It was marginal land, used and neglected and given over to kids and occasional walkers like themselves. Mick felt encouraged by the fact that no one would ever build more houses here. It would be as it had been. More so.

'That smell,' said Steve. 'Christ, it's like being a kid – it's like gone-off milk. And smoke.'

'And shit. And something else that might be sex.'

'It's a den, man, this is. It's all right if you're twelve, but it's no place for grown ups.'

'I think we've fallen through the cracks.' *At least you have,* thought Mick.

'I'm meant to get my bus pass next year,' said Steve. 'Give us a can. Mick took off his rucksack and pulled out a lager. He offered it to Steve.

'You not having one?'

'Not now. I suppose I'll have to drive us back as well, will I?'

'You southern ponce.' Steve coughed richly, then drank most of the can in one. 'I feel like shit, man, knorramean. After all that yesterday.'

'Get some sea breezes.'

'Not much breeze in here. It's like a fooking badger's khazi.'

The path descended among trees fantastically knotted and stooped against the wind, and the smell of smoke went with them. Kids had been lighting fires. Mick wondered what else there was to do out here. It wasn't exactly *Swallows and Amazons*. More like the Wood of Suicides. Which was not a useful thought, nor one to pass on to Steve.

Now Steve was behind him, pulling another can from the rucksack. Mick hadn't seen him finish the first but the new one disappeared double quick.

This had been a bad idea, thought Mick. He had encouraged Steve to do as Jules asked, and now he seemed to be stuck with it. Anyway, what choice was there? Crack on and get to the Point. Take a photo. Then get away.

'I don't like nature,' said Steve. 'I'm against nature, me.'

'This isn't nature.'

'What is it, then?'

'I dunno. Nowhere.' Mick shook his head. Steve was holding the rest of the cans by a plastic loop and finishing the third one.

'Steady on. I don't want to be carrying you back to the car.'

'Jules liked a drink,' said Steve, stumbling over a root. Mick could see the grief rising up in him, ageing him as they walked.

'More's the pity.'

'We didn't know, though, did we, back then? Nobody knew. It was just what you did. No harm in it. Few ales on a night.' *Here we go,* thought Mick. *Tears before bedtime.* 'I mean.'

'And the rest…'

'We were kids, though.'

'Never too young to get damaged.'

'You were there as well. You were into it.'

'I was lucky. Not like some.'

'You can't blame me,' said Steve.

It's not up to me to forgive you, Mick thought.

'I'm not blaming you,' he said. They had stopped walking. 'I'm not. I'm just saying how it was. Right?'

Steve nodded, looking at the ground.

'She was fucking beautiful, man, my Jules. She had light shining through her, man, clear white light.' That was part of the problem.

'Yes, she had.'

Steve's shoulders began to shake. Mick had to get away, if only for a minute. 'Wait here. I need a piss.' He moved off down another path. The low branches meant he had to stoop.

There was no point both of them cracking up. Mick squeezed his eyes shut.

The past seemed to have been waiting in the fort, almost intact. It had been summer, that time, the one Steve seemed not to remember. A group of them, him and Steve, Jules and her pal Shirley and two or three others, had come out here in the Transit and taken whatever was to hand. After that the group gradually separated as whatever they were using took hold.

In those days the landspit hadn't yet begun to succumb to longshore drift and wasn't washed over, so the road to the Point was obvious beneath the drifting sand. He'd come along the shore to the Point until he reached the fort. It was wooded even then, not so thickly but still private. There didn't seem to be anyone about when he scrambled up the hill and down into the bowl where the old goods line ran through the gates to supply the garrison. It was one of those warm, grey days he associated with childhood summers. Now he went further into the wood. *I'm not looking,* he told himself, *not really.*

It was an assignation, though nothing had been said. He had met her waiting where two paths crossed, and they went on in silence for a while until she took his hand and pulled him aside. They lay down in the shaded lee of a bunker. Once they heard voices nearby and above, laughter, someone calling, and they lay still, grinning at each other, transfigured by fear and desire, until the danger passed and she drew him in.

Afterwards, holding him tightly, she said, 'We can't do this again. You know that, don't you? It would kill him.'

'What about me?' Mick asked. She tilted her head wryly, smiled and shrugged, as though this was simply how it was and there was no more to be said, then gathered him into a long kiss.

'Anyway, you're off to university after the summer. And you've got Carol, haven't you?' she said.

'It's not what I want.'

'I know, love. But you must see.' She sat up. 'We ought to find the others. And we can't arrive back together.'

Half an hour later everyone was back at the Transit, dying of thirst, competing to be the most out of it.

You cannot live on scraps for forty years, he thought. Now Steve appeared on the path. 'I thought you'd fucked off.'

'No, just thinking,' said Mick. They moved on. Uphill now. There was the faint sound of the sea.

'It was good that some of them from the old days turned up last night,' said Steve.

'We're from the old days too.'

Jules had been adamant that she wouldn't leave Steve. They'd been together since schooldays. 'All the more reason,' said Mick. 'You'd don't understand,' she said. 'Well, tell me.' All she could do was give that sad shrug. 'It would kill Steve.' 'It's killing me,' said Mick. Despite what she said, they kept meeting. All they ever did was make love. They couldn't go for a walk or to the pictures or the pub. All that summer until Mick moved away. That stopped it, except in his head.

Then, somehow, it was years later. He was married and divorced and only came back now and then as a visitor at the university and when he did he went round. Same street, same house, the passage of time written in her face. The bottle of red open from noon on the kitchen table where she sat looking out into the yard while they talked. Steve was at the aircraft factory, then at the caravans, then in the quarry, then using his redundancy to start up as a spark. His van. The east end of the city. When Mick went round Steve was always out somewhere on a job.

They didn't go upstairs, didn't talk about it. She never moved house, no garden, no kids, no need. Never did the Fine Art course. Just the power of endurance, a bond honoured. Mick pretended to help her drink the red.

In the evening when Steve was back they went to the local. The last time, Mick left early, pleading a meeting first thing. Neither she nor Steve was coherent by the time he went. She didn't write and neither did he. More time, no end of it.

The visits seemed to have lapsed of their own accord until Steve got in touch. 'She's in Castle Hill,' he said. Anyone local knew what that meant. 'So if you want to see her, you know –' Mick said he'd try. He didn't. He waited until the news came. He couldn't get to the funeral, thankfully. He was going to let it go. Months passed. Then Mick texted him to say there was a memorial do at the club, with loads of people from the old days, and everyone wanted Mick to be there. Jules would have wanted it. They should all be together. And that was last night, the survivors clinging to the wreckage of undeserved good humour. There was a band, a buffet, the odd speech, far too much to drink, and lots of confused, tearful, hilarious feelings that grew maudlin and bitter as the drinks wore on. Mick helped carry Steve home.

The wood kept transferring them from path to path without releasing them. Now Steve had the half-bottle of vodka out of the rucksack. His face was lit up, cherry red, his eyes muffled somehow.

'We can't be bloody lost,' said Steve. He was slurring again. 'It's not big enough.'

'Up here, I think,' said Mick, moving ahead. Suddenly the wood was at an end and they reached the far rim of the fort. Under a sudden vast sky, the sloping shore was pebbles, mud, big branches brought down river then cast back up. The tide was strengthening, and with the wind coming from the east there was a jagged, shifting ridge in the water where the river met the sea. Some way out, the old military prison at Dog Island was just visible, rising like an oil platform. The huge dimming light and noise of it all seemed to swallow them up.

'This is it, is it?' said Steve, walking heavily down the beach. 'This is the Point?'

'Nowhere left to go, so it must be.' Across the wide mouth of the estuary the strange Sienese tower rose from flat greyness on the far shore. Container ships waited to enter and leave. River of the future they were calling it.

'She was a diamond,' said Steve, his face slick with tears. 'My Jules. Where are you? You were my diamond.' *And you hid her away and let her ruin herself,* thought Mick, afraid now that he might speak aloud and not notice. And she let it happen, let all the chances slide, and I bet you never even noticed, because there she was every day when you got back, as if that was where she wanted to be. And what did you give her? Fuck all. And what did I do about it? Fuck all. And what does that make us? A pair of sad fucking cunts.

'So this is where she meant?' Steve looked round, bemused.

'That's what you said she told you.'

'But why here? I mean.'

'I don't know, do I? But it seems to have been what she wanted.'

'Have you got it?'

'Of course.'

'Well, then.' Steve drank from the bottle. Mick took off the rucksack, opened it and took out the urn. 'Oh, fuck, man.' Steve put the urn under his arm. It was deep brown, made of some material like Bakelite.

'Come on, Steve. We've got to do it for her.'

'I can't, man, I can't.'

'Calm down.'

'How'm I meant to do that? She was everything. Oh, Jesus.'

'I know, Stevie, but she's gone now and we've got to honour her wishes.'

'You do it, then.'

'She was your wife.'

'I know but I can't.' They had come to the water's edge now. Steve sat down heavily on the wet mud. 'Do it for us, will you, Mick?'

'I know it's very hard, but it's what she wanted.'

'Fuck off. She never wanted to leave me.' Steve stared at him with grief and fury. 'Never.'

'I know. But this is in her honour. To show your love.'

'Can't you do it?'

Mick took the urn and walked a few paces. The colourless water licked at his shoes and slid back.

'You're sure? It should be you.'

'No, I want you to do it. Jules would understand.'

'Yes, she would, that's right.' Mick unscrewed the lid. 'OK, then.' The pale coarse ash sat in a clear plastic bag with a seal like a Ziploc. 'Do you want to say anything?'

'How do you mean?'

'A few words. A prayer.'

'I don't know any, do I? You do it.' It was like dealing with a child.

'I'll let the ashes be carried upriver on the wind, OK?'

'Is that all right, do you think?' asked Steve.

'They'll... she'll... get washed back to sea anyway, I suppose.' He put the urn down, opened the seal of the bag and stood to release the contents over the water. 'We say goodbye to our dear friend Jules, who's left us all too soon, and... and we wish her peace.' He began to tilt the bag.

'No, stop,' said Steve. 'Mick, stop.' He came unsteadily over and took the bag, carefully resealing it despite his shaking hands, then replacing it in the urn and putting the top on. Then he carried the urn back to the rucksack and packed it away. He put the rucksack on his back. 'It's not what she meant. Can't have been. I just wasn't listening, right? I was pissed or something. I got it wrong.' He set off back up the beach and into the woods.

Then they were back at the car. Steve sat with the rucksack clenched between his knees while Mick drove. They passed through the gateway at the landward end of the Point, then turned inland, running for a while along the edge of the mudflats. The tide was reclaiming the estuary now as the day darkened.

'I mean, it can't have been what she wanted,' Steve said. Mick shrugged. Steve uncapped the vodka bottle, took a drink and offered the bottle to Mick. Mick shook his head. 'I don't think that was it, anyway,' Steve went on. 'I misunderstood. Anyway, she was ill when she said it, right, man? So, you know, yeah?'

The lighthouse slid from view and the road moved inland between tall hedgerows. Mick put on the headlights. He nodded. 'Yeah, OK, Steve. I know. It's OK.'

'Thanks, man. You're a friend, knorramean.'

Ex Libris

GUZMAN FOUND HIMSELF DESCENDING a ladder in a circular concrete shaft. The gloom prevented him from seeing how far he had come or how far there was to go. The shaft itself seemed to be sweating, and the rungs of the ladder were wrapped in what seemed to be old carpet. At times the fabric slipped against the metal. *My name is Guzman*, he realised. That was all. There seemed nothing for it but to continue his descent.

Guzman had no watch, but his downward passage seemed to go on for hours. At last he stopped and wrapped his arms around the vertical poles of the ladder. The muscles of his legs and back were burning. For a while he hung there trying to think, but whatever state he was trying to recall or produce evaded him. He had woken on the ladder; on the ladder he remained. He had gone too far to turn back, but where would it end? Perhaps he could simply let go and fall. As this thought surfaced, something brushed against his shoulder. Startled, he saw a magpie beating its wings and vanishing into the murk below. The only thing, he supposed, was to follow the creature downwards, if downwards was the word for it.

The bird created an expectation that for a further extended period it seemed would find no fulfilment. There was the sweating shaft, the ladder, the descent. After a time he scarcely thought, scarcely registered the discomfort of his futile progress. A scrap of a song ran round his head: *I am a man of constant sorrow/ I've seen trouble all my day*. Then, before he knew it, he reached the bottom of the shaft, lowering himself to the final rung before dropping a few feet onto a flat area of uncertain but vast extent.

The ground of this place (if those were either of the words) was composed of what seemed to be the covers of innumerable books of all sizes, their titles displayed in many languages. He noticed, randomly, *Effi Briest*, *The Zaragoza Manuscript*, *Gentlemen Prefer Blondes*, *Elective Affinities*, *Melmoth the Wanderer*, and there grew in him the recognition that what he was feeling was an indictment as far as he could see in all directions, fading into a haze. What they had in common, the titles his eye had fallen on, was he suspected that he had not read them. It seemed reasonable to infer that this only mattered because he was in some way bookish, or literary, himself. At some prior but undisclosed point he had nursed the intention to read them, and now he was here with everything at his disposal, and it amounted to an indictment of his bad faith. There is something metaphysical about this, thought Guzman. A blast of pain passed through his head as if in confirmation.

He moved gingerly away from the shaft, then turned to see the ladder slowly withdrawing into the low cloud which formed the ceiling of the vast plain. He raised a hand as if to appeal for its return but his most powerful feeling was exhaustion. With an instinct to find shelter, he opened a huge book. Without registering the cover, he lay down and let the book half-close on him. In the dry, slightly foxed light he found himself reading the foot-high opening sentences of *Leviathan*. Soon he fell asleep.

How long he had slept he could not tell. He awoke with a terrible thirst and the certainty that there was no water to be had in this plain of paper. He climbed out of the book and stood up, peering about. In his pocket he found a stub of pencil and a scrap of paper on which was written: *No Gloves for the Hangman* by Zeke Allison, Rockhampton, Rockhampton Press, 1947. So, then, it was a quest, for a book he had never heard of, never mind read. What kind of book? A western, perhaps – but surely Rockhampton was in Australia. Guzman sighed. He would die of thirst in this desert of print, this plain with 'nothing to eat and nowhere to sit down'. The quotation whispered through his mind without attribution. The pain in his head returned. He heard the wingbeat of the magpie just before it brushed his shoulder. It landed twenty yards or so away, and turned to face him before taking off once more. There seemed no reason not to follow.

For a long time the bird maintained its routine, flying a little way, turning to look, flying again, while Guzman trudged in its wake. The titles and the authors changed but the horizontal plain did not. Guzman's head ached with dryness. Had he possessed any equipment he would have discarded it. His gaze was drawn to the random catalogue beneath his feet. Montesquieu, Manzoni, Hank Janson, Elinor Glyn, Jacqueline Susann, Pushkin, *The Times Atlas of the World*. Although he knew that to start reading or even browsing now would be fatal, he knelt down beside the book to open it, and to his surprise he was able to lift it out of position. Beneath it lay a clear pane of water. It might be salt but Guzman did not care. He lay down and drank as though to drain an ocean.

When at last he raised his head he found the magpie in close attendance. It gestured with one wing like someone indicating a wristwatch. Restored, Guzman set off once more behind the bird. At least there was water. And something to read. To put it mildly. He laughed aloud but then began to think about the odds against happening on a copy of *No Gloves for the Hangman* in this uncatalogued biblio-world.

So preoccupied was Guzman with reading the titles and authors' names that he did not at first register that a fog had begun to form. The bird was only intermittently visible.

Guzman hastened on. Then through the fog, snow began to fall and with it the temperature. The bird had vanished.

Feeling his way forward over the thickening crust of snow, Guzman tripped on a displaced book. When he rose the ground seemed to have become unsteady. Then a gap appeared between the two volumes on which he stood, and black water lapped at the pages. He moved to stand on a single book the size of a paving stone. It tilted alarmingly beneath him and glimpsing a larger volume drifting past he jumped and lay full length. Now he heard the sound of waves. He spread himself on a vast copy of *Moby Dick*, like Ishmael clinging to Queequeg's coffin. He would either drown or freeze to death. He prayed to be relieved of consciousness. His prayer was answered and he sank into dreamlessness.

He was awoken by voices. He looked up and found that the snow had stopped and he was still afloat on the book-berg in a field of similar snow-covered volumes, slowly moving on the inky water. The fog too had cleared but the sky remained low and grey. The magpie was nowhere to be seen. Then, once again, he heard voices, this time raised. He got carefully to his feet and peered around him. Directly ahead a rowing boat came into view. He made out two figures, one with its back to him rowing, the other standing up and peering through a telescope. They seemed to be wearing tricorn hats. The gaze of the telescope fell on him. The watching figure stooped and then straightened up holding a musket.

'What are you, sir?' came the loud voice of the standing figure. 'A privateer? A Portugee?' The boat came steadily closer. The bewigged figure cocked the weapon. His companion shipped the oars and turned with a pistol in his hand.

'Neither of those things,' said Guzman, surprised by the sound of his own voice. 'I am lost.'

'To be lost covers a multitude of sins, sir. You must offer

an account of yourself. We have met such as you before.'

'I have no memory,' said Guzman. 'I have simply found myself in this place, if it is a place. Only regrets and desires remain to me.'

'What is your name?'

'My name?' Now the Christian name supplied itself too. 'My name is Raimund Guzman.'

'A Spaniard, then.' The taller figure nodded as if this might have been expected.

'I don't know what I am. I ask you not to shoot me,' Guzman said. 'I am not armed. I am lost and in search of shelter and an explanation.'

'Are you a Christian fellow?'

'I cannot answer that. I have no information to give you. I found myself climbing down a ladder on to a plain of books. I walked and the plain began to break up into these bergs. I slept. And now I meet you.'

'He is likely a djinn,' said the oarsman, in a Scottish accent, turning to his companion. 'If we shoot him the charge will make smoke of him, Doctor. If not, I fear he will make smoke of us.'

'Be quiet, Boswell. I am thinking.' Boswell shook his head. The boat had drifted very near now. At length the Doctor put down his weapon 'Let him aboard. He can share your labours at the oars.'

'I do not think it wise, Dr Johnson,' said Boswell.

'I do not think *you* wise,' said the Doctor. 'But I hold my tongue about it, do I not? Put up your weapon, sir.' Boswell shrugged and put his pistol away, then reached out a hand to assist Guzman into the vessel. It was, Guzman thought, too large for one man to row easily, though he doubted if the Doctor shared in Boswell's labours. A mast and sail lay unused, and the prow and all other spaces and crannies were stowed with bags and chests. His companions seemed strangely familiar, but their names meant nothing to him, though his persisting depression and guilt suggested that they should.

'Sit down, sir,' said the Doctor. He was a man of remarkable ugliness, his vast face pitted with some affliction. His black coat and breeches were shiny with use and he stank in a way that made Guzman catch his breath. Boswell, diminutive in comparison, seemed untroubled by the smell and was not entirely sweetness himself. 'Get food for our guest, Boswell.' The little man busied himself in one of the canvas bags and produced a stony loaf and a hunk of ancient meat which he put on a plate. These he handed to Guzman along with a bottle of Geneva. His task complete, he took out a writing case and a notebook and sat expectantly at Guzman's side.

'You are a man without a story,' said the Doctor. 'Perhaps there is no diversion to be got out of you.' Boswell wrote this down.

'I apologise,' said Guzman. 'Except that I can recognise books and that there seem to be none here that I have read, I am at a loss. But it seems that you and your companion do not share this trouble, Doctor.'

'We share the gifts reserved for age,' said the Doctor, seeming to take recognition for granted. 'I warrant you that is trouble enough. We labour like you in hope's delusive mine.'

'I do not think this is a mine,' said Guzman.

'I speak in figures, sir,' said the Doctor, drinking from the Geneva bottle before firmly replacing the stopper, 'being part-poet, for my sins.'

'The Doctor has many strings to his bow,' added Boswell, and would have said more had his master not stopped him with a glance.

'Since I can offer nothing of use,' said Guzman, 'can you enlighten me?'

'We have retained our histories and our names and, as you

see, a fine balance between flattery and contempt. But as to how Boswell and I came here, it is all a darkness.'

'Inspissated gloom,' muttered Boswell, sharpening a fresh quill.

'At one moment we were seated in the chop-house with Addison and Steele – I can see that these names will mean nothing to you – the next we were aboard our little craft, and have been so a week now. I may add that I have no appetite for adventure. To have travelled in the highlands and islands gave me sufficient sight of the world. But here we are and here we must endure.' The Doctor turned away, unbuttoned his breeches and urinated into the inky waters.

'Faith endures,' muttered Boswell, scratching away.

'Damme, sir, am I to strike you?' roared the Doctor.

'But who will row your vessel then?' said the little man, slyly.

'Then fall to it,' said the Doctor. 'Matters are not improved by our remaining here.' Guzman and Boswell took up the oars and pulled away through the bookish waste. Conversation lapsed and the Doctor began to read aloud from the Books of Ecclesiastes and Job. It was weary work, Guzman found, and the reading tended to lower his spirits further. He ached, he longed to sleep, but after a time he fell into a trance produced by the rhythm of the oars and his own deep exhaustion.

When Guzman next took thought it was dark. The Doctor stood in the prow with a lantern trying to guide their passage. The books seemed fewer and vaster, as though they were coming nearer to one of the poles of whatever dreadful place this was.

'We should rest,' said Boswell.

'Quiet,' said his master. 'There is something out there.' As he spoke, the waters beside them seemed to erupt, and Guzman saw something vast breaking swiftly through the surface. At first he thought it might be a whale, but insofar as he could make it out the thing seemed ironclad. It reared as if it must crush them, then just as suddenly settled, revealing itself as a vast submarine, its ribs and plates studded with huge rivets. There was the sound of hatches thrown open. A powerful lamp was aimed into the rowing boat from the conning tower. Once more the Doctor aimed his musket.

'It is useless to resist,' declared a voice from a loud hailer. 'Put down your weapons. For you the war is over. Abandon hope all you who enter here.'

'Do as he says,' urged Guzman.

'Heterogeneous ideas —' said the Doctor.

'— Yoked by violence together,' Boswell replied. The pair set down their guns.

The magpie perched on the end of the iron bedstead, a silver chain about its foot. Deep in the bowels of the craft, the cell was extremely hot, running with condensation, but a handsome cast-iron drinking fountain provided a supply of fresh water. The trio sat and looked about them. The noise of the submerging craft had faded now.

'Have I gone mad, Boswell?' asked the Doctor. 'I would not be mad.'

'You are brushed by the wing of madness merely,' the scribe replied. 'Or I am mad, and Master Guzman and the great world are mad likewise.'

'I think we are travelling beneath the sea,' said the Doctor. 'It is against nature. Men are not gods or nymphs to delve in Neptune's pastures.'

'The ship is mechanical,' said Guzman. 'It has some form of power that enables us to breathe in its confinement, and we can sense its movement. There is nothing supernatural about this.'

'Are you a literary man?' the Doctor asked Guzman.

'I think somehow I may have been. What makes you ask?'

'The thought simply occurred to me,' said the Doctor. 'It also occurs to me that our present plight may have rather more to do with you than with myself or Boswell.'

'We are blameless, I think,' said Boswell, busying himself with his notebook again. 'But you, sir, what have you done to bring us to this?'

'I wish I knew,' Guzman muttered, beginning to dislike the small Scotsman.

The three fell to brooding, listening uneasily to the clangs and hisses of the great vessel. Occasionally footsteps came and went in the corridor outside. At length the Doctor produced a clay pipe from his voluminous coat and set to work to light it. As soon as smoke was produced a loud alarm went off and lights began to flash.

A key sounded in the lock and the studded metal door swung inwards. A pair of black-uniformed Cyclopses wearing caps with lightning flashes gestured for the Doctor to extinguish his pipe and then marched the trio through the boiling bowels of the great submarine until at last they ascended a spiral staircase and found themselves in a lavishly appointed study with a vast curved window that looked out into the dark ocean. Unidentifiable but tentacular creatures flickered in and out of view, drawn by the lit interior.

Terrible music was playing. Guzman saw a black-clad figure seated at a vast church organ, leaning back from time to time as though in passion, while grandiose discords sprang from its fingers like a series of violent mechanical accidents. *He is pretending to be able to play,* thought Guzman.

As though overhearing this, the figure ceased its labours, rose and turned to greet his guests. Like the crew, he wore a dark uniform, to which was added a cap clearly indicating high rank, its insignia incorporating the lightning flash on a twisted cross of some kind. The man – if such he was – also wore an eyeless black balaclava with a hole left for the mouth.

'Dr Johnson, Mr Boswell, Guzman. Good evening, gentlemen. I have been expecting you.'

'You have the advantage of us, sir,' said Dr Johnson.

'Indeed,' said the masked figure. 'Knowledge is power.'

'Power being yours, might you offer us the courtesy of your name?' The dark figure nodded, raising a black-gloved hand to his black chin as though considering.

'Captain Erich Von Nemo at your service. For this evening, you are my guests. Come, let us eat.' At this waiters appeared with chafing dishes and the Captain led the party to a long table laid with napery and silver cutlery.

'Do you understand the uses of knives and forks, Mr Guzman?' asked the Captain when they were seated.

'I am indifferent to them,' Guzman replied, weighing a heavy fish-knife in his palm.

'Food is an index of civilisation', said the Captain. He gestured to the waiters who began serving from the dishes. From where he was sitting Guzman saw the organ continuing to play quietly, but still tunelessly, by itself. When he looked down at his plate a long vegetable of luminous green lay twitching and steaming on a bed of weed and white sauce.

'Eat, gentlemen. The deep ocean provides us with all the nutrition we need.' He sawed his food into several pieces and inserted them in the black slot of his mouth.

Experimentally, Guzman stabbed the thing. With a sigh of steam it deflated, releasing an ooze in a darker shade of green. He noticed that the Doctor and Boswell were contenting themselves with bread. He took a piece and nibbled. It was like nothing he had ever eaten. The wine was green and salty. He poured himself some water and moved the food around his plate before secreting the knife in his pocket. It struck him that there was not a single book to be seen in the room. The walls were decorated with paintings of Captain Nemo in various attitudes of marine heroism, as, he noticed, were the placemats.

'I feel I must ask,' Guzman said, 'though I can see that it is not your field, whether you can help me with the quest I seem to be on.' The Captain inclined his head.

'Of what nature is this quest?'

'I am searching for a book. But I infer you are not bookish.'

'Quite the contrary,' said the Captain. 'What was the book?'

'*No Gloves for the Hangman* by Zeke Allison.'

'It sounds like a work by Karl May,' the Captain declared. 'But here we are done with all that, done with the delusions of literature.'

'A man who loves not books is a dog in human form,' declared the Doctor.

'Wait. I must write that down,' said Boswell. 'Have you any paper, Captain?'

'Oh, yes,' the Captain replied, reaching for a bell-pull. 'I am well supplied with paper. In fact I consume a great deal of it, as you will see.' A concealed door opened with a hiss and half a dozen black-uniformed Cyclops-sailors entered, heavily armed.

'I should add that I myself am not *especially* fond of books,' said Guzman as the party dragged him and his companions from the room and down a further series of corridors deeper into the vessel. The noise intensified to a fiery roar. At length they came to the vast engine room, the size of a cathedral, where bare-chested crewmen scurried beneath the violent movements of huge steel pistons. It was infernally hot. By some means the Captain was there before them, looking down on them from a railed balcony.

'Show these gentlemen how we power the engines,' said the Captain. Approaching on a narrow-gauge railway across the vast iron floor was a self-propelling vehicle the size of a touring coach, a tender of some kind. Its driver halted before a vast set of iron doors which now slid open to reveal the red glare of a furnace. The heat worsened. The Captain nodded and the tender began to tilt on hydraulic legs, revealing its contents to the watching trio. Books, tons of books, thousands on thousands of books, sliding into the hungry flames.

'The ocean, gentlemen – the ocean provides for all our needs. It is food, it is fuel, and it is cultural purgation! Death to the book, the book that has ensnared us so long with its sick enchantments. We have an ocean to burn.'

'You are a barbarian, sir,' declared the Doctor, his expression stricken with grief.

'That being so, how do you think I will respond to your puny taunts?' asked the Captain. He nodded once more and the guards seized the Doctor and Boswell, dragged them screaming to the furnace and hurled them into the flames. Their cries were snatched away in the blinding light and the furnace doors slid shut once more. Guzman, unable to believe his eyes, stood in shock. The Captain descended from the balcony and stood beside him.

'Oh, yes,' said the Captain. 'I can and I will.'

'Who would dispute it?' asked Guzman bitterly.

'War is hell.'

'And so it seems is literature.'

'It is all lies and rhetoric and purple fog. It neither affirms nor denies. But it burns – which makes it useful. I could fuel this vessel for millennia and make no impact on the mountains of accursed books that folly has permitted to accumulate.'

'Why have you not killed me like my companions?'

'Good question.' For a moment Captain Nemo's outline, and the pipework and ducts and busy figures behind him, seemed to lose their outline and definition. Guzman blinked. Nemo nodded to the guards. 'Take him to my cabin.'

The Captain's quarters were private and spartan and, it appeared, wholly bookless. Despairing and exhausted, Guzman lay down on the bunk and fell into a dreamless sleep. It may have been the silence that awoke him at last. The silence was complete, as if the vessel had stopped and with it all the scurrying work of the crew. Guzman sat up and felt for the knife. It was still in his pocket. That was something. So far he had been spared by the unexplained whim of Nemo. I must act, he told himself, in the interests of self-preservation, if only to find out what is going on and what it means.

To the right of Nemo's desk stood a small safe of the kind that Guzman seemed to recognise as useful in storing confidential documents – not that Nemo would have any of those in his paperless office. Idly, Guzman tried the handle. The safe swung open. *Well, of course*, he found himself thinking. All it contained was a single black book. He went to the door and looked up and down the corridor. No one there and no sound. He went back and took the book from the safe: an old clothbound hardback entitled *No Gloves for the Hangman*. The fulfilment of his quest, though he felt more like a patient than an agent in this matter. He opened the book and turned to the opening page. Might as well have a read as do anything else.

The opening page was a pane of clear water. Guzman tipped the book on end but the water stayed put. He dipped a finger in and the water was undisturbed. He closed the book and opened it again. The water stared blankly back. Then, as though from the depths it could not possibly possess, a face rose slowly towards the surface and halted, barely submerged.

'Remember me?' The face was a man's, in late middle age, drawn and jaundiced, with thinning colourless hair.

'No, I'm sorry. Should I?'

'Oh, yes,' said the man. He nodded and a blast of pain travelled through Guzman's head. When his vision cleared, he had to admit that the underwater figure did strike a faint chord.

'How about now?' the man asked.

'Very vaguely. Are you –' The pain came again, more intensely, and as though precisely engineered to make Guzman's teeth explode and his eyeballs burst.

'You are unable to put it down,' said the man. 'That is not what you found in the case of my book, however, was it, Mr Guzman, or should I say cunt?'

'Sorry, what book?'

'What book? You dare to ask me that?' More pain, the top of the spinal column turning to lava and bubbling into Guzman's mouth.

'I'm sorry. I don't know what you're talking about. Or who you are. Or where this place is, if it is a place. Why are you tormenting me?'

'Go out into the corridor and look around. Explore.'

'They won't let me.'

'Don't be so sure. You will have to take "me" with you, of course.'

Once again Guzman put his head round the door. No one. He retraced his steps to the engine room. It was silent and in semi-darkness. There was a stench of rotting fish. There seemed be no one about – that is, until he found himself standing on crew uniforms scattered about the floor.

'Look more closely,' said the man in the pane of water. Guzman crouched to examine one of the uniforms. When he lifted up the shirt, opaque grey slime, like tapioca pudding or frogspawn, flowed from the sleeves of the garment. For this first time, Guzman found himself gripped by horror.

'What has happened to them?'

'Curious, is it not?' said the face, delivering another charge of pain. 'Now make your way to the Captain's dining room.' The corridors were dimming slowly. Here and there Guzman encountered piles of slumped rags leaking grey filth. After a time he found the spiral staircase and ascended to the dining room. Here too it was dim. A low discord was very slowly fading. The Captain, or whatever he had been, had slumped across the keyboard, and as his bogus substance melted from his clothes the keys of the organ were gradually returning to a silent position. As Guzman sought to register this, the book released itself from his hand to hang suspended at head height. In doing so it grew larger, and the face beneath the water became life-size and declared:

> Our revels now are ended. These our actors,
> As I foretold you, were all spirits and
> Are melted into air, into thin air:
> And, like the baseless fabric of this vision,
> The cloud-capp'd towers, the gorgeous palaces,
> The solemn temples, the great globe itself,
> Yea, all which it inherit, shall dissolve
> And, like this insubstantial pageant faded,
> Leave not a rack behind. We are such stuff
> As dreams are made on, and our little life
> Is rounded with a sleep.

The face regarded Guzman calmly now.

'You must remember this.'

'Oh, yes,' said Guzman. 'Of course. Everybody knows those lines.'

'Let's not exaggerate,' said the face. Guzman flinched in anticipation of more pain. The face smiled. 'I am not a monster,' it declared.

'Then what are you?'

'An avatar.'

'What?'

'And so are you. An avatar. We are the imagined representatives of ourselves in the space of the imagination. Digital doubles.'

'Then where is the real me?'

'Asleep in my basement in an induced coma.'

'A coma into which you put me.'

'Correct, Mr Guzman.' Guzman knew what was coming. The burst of agony flung him across the room and against the dining table. The face in the book followed to where he lay and looked down.

'Why am I doing this?' asked the face. 'Because my name is Hanno Biedermeier. Because I am a novelist and you purport to be a critic. Because in the everyday analogue world you wrote destructively and contemptuously about my work. Because I am rich and can enlist others to do my virtual bidding and put you here with amnesia while your physical, your real self, sleeps on forgotten by the world you sought to amuse with your insulting bon mots and the perpetual suggestion that you, though not a novelist, knew infinitely better when it came to novels than a mere novelist such as myself, and that what I have spent a lifetime writing, is no better than a cheap Australian western printed on austerity lavatory paper. Is anything coming back to you?' Guzman propped himself in a chair.

'Yes, now you mention it. But Biedermeier, I assure you that it was not from personal animus that I wrote. It was my obligation as a critic – as I saw it then – to attack what seemed to me to be bad work, such as – please don't hurt me any more – such as yours. No personal offence was intended. You have to take it on the chin. That's the game.'

'Game? In the sense that this here – this elaborate confection of illusion – is a game?'

'Not quite. I was speaking figuratively.'

'You were not,' Biedermeier said in a level tone. 'You were speaking as a fool, and look where your foolishness has brought you, to a world which is indeed entirely foolish, where nothing is substantial and only your suffering is real. A place of misquotation, misremembering, inappositeness, anachronism, of confusion of genres and of seriousness with vulgar entertainment, of muddle and laziness and evasion and shallowness – in short, and if I may term it so, a digital analogue of your own interior mediocrity.'

'What happens now?'

'Look about you.'

Black water was beginning to well up at the head of the spiral staircase, spreading, silently for now, across the carpet to Guzman's feet.

'We're sinking,' said Guzman.

'No, Guzman, you are sinking. I am elsewhere. And in this place you are no more real than anything else.'

'But I feel real,' said Guzman. The water lapped at his ankles.

'I imagine you do.' By some means Biedermeier switched himself off and disappeared, and Guzman tried to remember the whereabouts of the hatch by which he had entered the submarine. Not that it mattered, since it was, as Biedermeier had said, only a game, though the water was convincingly cold as it washed against his legs. He felt disinclined to move, and out of the soup of circumstance and illusion there came to him a quotation from a poem he had read in early youth and set great store by:

This last pain for the damned the Fathers found:
'They knew the bliss with which they were not crowned
Such, but on earth, let me foretell,
Is all, of heaven or of hell.'

The lines of the poem were accompanied by an image of a man sitting under a tree on a sunny hillside reading a book for no other reason than pleasure. Guzman sighed at the idea, but then the book in the reader's hand began to shout at him, and lightning struck the tree, and an earthquake occurred, and the tide of ink rose, very convincingly Guzman thought, over Guzman's mouth, his nose and his head.

Story Time

June 1ST

It is early summer. There is a metalled single-lane road that turns into a track and tilts downhill into the woods. Once I am in the woods the water becomes visible, a great reach of it with a scatter of islands. I suspect – I have no map – that the large forested area a quarter of a mile away may itself be an island, which in turn provokes the possibility that where I stand might be an island too. But this cannot be so, surely. I seem to remember that I arrived overland.

At the foot of the track is a clearing set back a little way from the water's edge, and in the clearing are standing a whitewashed farm cottage and one or two half-derelict looking sheds. A tabby cat slinks away at my approach and watches from behind a birch tree.

Although it is summer a curl of smoke rises from the cottage chimney. The door is open. I knock but no one answers. Hesitantly I put my head round the door. Beyond lies the dim kitchen – the heavy varnished table with its loaf and board and knife, a family Bible with a place marked deep in the Old Testament, the deep fireplace giving out slightly too much heat, the ugly dresser with its ugly carved flower-patterns. The whole apparatus of nameless provincial life, halfway between Balzac and Perrault. The clock, in pride of place on the dresser, ticks. It is just before noon. I look at the marked verse of scripture: *yea, also the heart of the sons of men is full of evil, and madness is in their heart while they live, and after that they go to the dead.*

On the far side of the kitchen a further door stands slightly open. It is clear what I must do, but this is as far as I want / feel able to go. I turn to leave.

June 3rd

'Mixing memory and desire.' Who said that? I should remember. But I should not desire and, ergo, should not remember, either.

The library is wholly inadequate to my requirements. I complain but go unheard. It is I who must change and not the place. Or so they say.

June 5th

I have never liked cats. They look as if they have greater seniority. They cry, they mate at the back of places, they sleep all day as if full of accomplishment. I approach the cat on the edge of the clearing. It walks away but does not run. It will not scare. I think of picking up a stone. I think of shouting, but my mouth remains clamped shut.

The birds are silent, I notice. Nothing moves on the vast reach whose water reflects the high clouds. Smoke still rises from the cottage chimney. I knock and no one answers. I enter and nothing is changed. I take a seat at the table. Since it would be rude to eat the loaf, I open the Bible at the page marked with a prayer card. *The wages of sin is death.*

That will do for today.

June 7th

I am fobbed off with entertainments, detective novels. Poetry is inadvisable, it seems. But I'm the sort of lad, the class of a boyo, who can find the poetry in Dick Francis. I wonder if anyone else has actually read this filth. Is this what you want of me, Doctor? Surely not. Orange with tranquillity, most of my sad companions are not in a position to read or indeed do anything for themselves, while the administrators like to think they have better things with which to occupy themselves. Over-promoted poseurs.

Since I rarely sleep I am rapidly exhausting the library's stock. What will happen when I do? Go over it again? Aren't we supposed to be getting away from all that? Isn't that the part we're 'trying to put behind us'? What if I fail? But if I fail, it will not be me who fails, will it, Doctor, not really? Another boy did it and ran away.

June 10th

A bad day. No stories today.

June 12th

Through the woods, down the gentle hill into the clearing. The cat is nowhere to be seen, though it can probably see *me*. The door is ajar, the kitchen empty, the fire winking redly, the loaf white and stiff as a cork float, like evidence and not food. Across the room the inner door stands slightly open. In the passage behind it I can see a broom leaning against the whitewashed wall. Neutral, open. And the Bible too is open where I left it on the table. *The wages of sin is death*. So the mood today is still proverbial, and the accompanying reading is of an improving, not to say threatening kind. *The wages of sin is death*: the phrase reminds me. I have forgotten to bring something. Or I have come here to the cottage in the clearing by the water for some purpose I cannot recall. I would like to thrust my hand into the fire like Latimer – was it Latimer? Is this something I should remember or not? – when they burnt him at the stake. I turn the heavy pages. *And I was sore afraid*. But I am not afraid. A little anxious, perhaps. But not afraid. Fear is elsewhere. I look into the fire for some time. I warm my hands. But I do not burn them. Why would I?

June 14th

It is wearisome to be treated as a fool by fools. Let us speak plainly. When I look under historical fiction I find *The Da Vinci Code*. Has anyone else read this, the 'work' of this 'Dan Brown', this obvious degenerate, this semi-literate petty criminal?

I ask again for poetry, but poetry is bad for me, and anyway, what poetry do I mean? You know, I say, that I do not remember. That is the point, is it not? How should I remember what I do not remember, O my Doctor? The idea, surely, is that I should not. There follows the smile, the reassurance professionals give each other, their sense of strength in numbers, as if their white-coated kind stretched in a great queue down an endless corridor waiting their turn to be in here, doing as their colleagues do. *Rather strangle an infant in its cradle than nurse an unfulfilled desire* speaks itself unbidden through my mouth. A note is made. It is clear that she does not recognise the source; but neither do I.

June 15th

The rustic scene has lost its charm. Metalled road becoming track, running downhill, clearing, wide water, whitewashed cottage, ruinous sheds, cat nailed over the lintel of the door with its head under its arm. In fact I made that last part up. Is that allowed?

I feel like an estate agent showing myself round a property I wouldn't dream of buying. I never dream now, not since the intervention. Blank nights, the strange deep blankness, as if everything were over or had never taken place. Perfection of a kind. Of my kind. Of my sort, knorramean?

Kitchen table, Bible, fire, dresser, proggy mat, hideous crockery, smoke-brown genre painting over the fireplace. Bags of potential, I'm sure I'll agree, for a young professional couple planning to set up as child murderers.

And the inner door. Yes, that. It hasn't gone away, still half-open with the broom behind it leaning on the whitewashed wall of the corridor. The scene itself is indifferent: act, don't act, it makes no odds to the scene, which is always here around this time, with the beautiful loaded neutrality of a detail in a picture by Chardin. Across the canvas the great silence of the woman writing a letter or the servant sewing goes on. But I know what is required of me. Go over. Stand by the doorway. I know that comes next. Don't spoil the party.

June 16th

You, Dr Murdoch, you, I see, are afraid. Oho. You are, I think, wise in this respect at least. You look at me slightly too long before you take your glasses off to tuck your long red hair behind your ear. You and I might make a connection, but I would bet money that you will be absent from the next session. Afraid. Everybody would be wise to be afraid, under the circumstances in which we find ourselves, whatever role is given us to play in this medical panopticon. It is a scene of crime – crime actual, crime dreamed on the brink of waking, crime planned with patient passion through the long dim afternoons. It leaks from the walls, does crime. You find its residue under your fingernails, on the cuffs of your blouse and the toes of your tights when you undress for bed in the tidy flat I can imagine in every detail. Crime. You know it makes sense.

Imagine this great building underwater, sealed and secure for centuries on the bed of a great lake, and then one afternoon a doctor – you, Dr Murdoch, for example – finds a patch of damp in a cellar corridor, and feels a skin of water growing patiently beneath her touch. By then the state is already undone. The prisoners in the deepest oubliettes have drowned in crime. Those who survive the inundation will be crime-drinkers, breathers of crime, mutations built for their element, the criminal depths, deeper than the Atlantic, deeper even than the bottomless city of Paris. Who said this? I don't remember. Me, perhaps.

I ask you for poetry. You give me pills to help me adapt to the changed conditions. To adapt to the adaptations. When I object, you are stung. You point at the books on your shelves – books you will not lend me – and tell me tersely that I am a machine driven by desire. Not any more, I say, not according to you. Not if it's worked. All that's supposed to be over with. A silence falls, not of your making. You struggle to claim it for yourself. I add a little goad: *Who is as the wise man? And who knoweth the interpretation of a thing?* Stop it, you say, I am trying to think.

What about belief? I ask. You shake your head. What about the spirit? You snort and make another note. We're done, you say, for today. But, surely, I am undone, Doctor? I am not that strength which once I was. My right arm has lost its cunning and my liver is damaged by the drugs I am given to help me adapt to the changed conditions, and there is nothing to fucking read. You suggest I play table tennis.

June 19th

The sky is white but where it meets the trees it has a slaty, purplish note. It is much too hot, but rain seems unlikely. The cat is in the rain barrel and the cottage smokes like a chimney. The door grates open, as if a piece of chalk has lodged under it. In the baking kitchen I sit at the table, feeling exhausted. A cauldron hangs from a hook, a hearty stew, the sort added to for weeks on end, bubbling with steady complacency like a mud-pool near a geyser you can set your watch by. It is noon. It has never been anything else. Flick the bread with a finger. It sounds like a de-tuned snare-drum.

Somebody has moved the broom from its place leaning on the whitewashed wall beyond the opened doorway. Now it stands against the dresser, tensed as if about to multiply. This fills me with anger. I feel so crammed with anger it might start leaking from under my fingernails. Whose business is it to move the broom? I was getting round to it in my own time. One has to build up to these things, to prepare to make one's move. Now I think I see what you would have me believe. I take the broom and go to the doorway. You would have me suppose that there is nothing beyond, that the patch of white wall is all that is the case, and otherwise nothing obtains. There is no corridor, there are no rooms leading off it, no beds and dressing-tables, and if it were possible to multiply an absence, even more certainly no*body* there. There never has been. Your will is to make me your creature, a wreckage of half-memories steering clear of the bad words until death intervenes to spare me further humiliation. All that was, is no more, shall be no more. I shall not think of it, shall not smell the smell of self at work in a further room.

It must be true, Dr Murdoch. You have squared the circle, seized the fire, found a cure for capitalism and brought cancer to its knees, downsized God and erased me from myself, leaving this tabula rasa, year zero, hollow man, to gibber harmlessly to himself and *not go back there or think of doing so*.

As you wish. All I do is place the broom back in its original position against the wall beyond the inner door. I do not look to either side. I feel no draught, smell no spoor, follow no line of association. I turn back to face the kitchen and go over to sit on a stool by the baking hearth. I take the lid from the cauldron, the heat stinging my palm, take up the iron ladle and stir. Your bald head surfaces, the eyes like bleary eggs, the skin slick with fat. I take a plastic spoon from my shirt pocket and begin to eat your brains with it. Are we done? Can I go now? You tell me. I can't remember.

Swan, 1914

LADIES AND GENTLEMEN, I shall not be here for long; and nor will you. Nature has taken its course. For many of us the mortal span is ended; for others death approaches swiftly. It must be so. I speak to you from my desk and those of you who live are, many of you, scattered across the globe, but let us entertain the notion that we are all present to each other this evening in the lecture theatre of the Literary and Philosophical Society – as we were present (numbering, it is said, seven hundred) on the night when I addressed you in this very room on 20th October 1880, Lord Armstrong in the chair. At the conclusion of my address I asked for the seventy gas jets which at that time illuminated the room to be turned off. Let us suppose that; let us endow ourselves with temporary immortality. Turn off the gas. Here we are, then, in the dark, are we not? – As in the darkness that lay on the face of the waters. Now then. Bear with my story. I shall be brief.

When I was a boy the poor went to bed at sunset and frightened their children with the bogeyman Bonaparte. My family was never quite poor, but our fortunes declined by stages because of my father's generosity and improvidence and his trusting nature. I most remember our house in Pallion looking down on to the wooded slopes and shipyards of the Wear. We children would sing our adaptation of a Methodist hymn:

And then we'll shout and shine and sing
And make the Pallion arches ring
When all the Swans come home.

I think I have spent my life attempting to come home.

We had to leave that house, and then another, and at last up sticks to Newcastle, but not before my curiosity led me into all the yards and workshops of the banks of the Wear to pursue my fascination with the physical processes of God's creation. 'And the light shineth in darkness; and the darkness comprehended it not', as John's Gospel states. It was often a dark world, but at that early date science gave me means to light my way.

As to my incandescent lightbulb, it was a process of many years of thought and experimentation that led me at last to solve the fundamental problem of the device: how to create a bulb that would not only convert electricity into light but do so over a sustained period, thus making the bulb a useful domestic object. As I remarked before, there is no invention that does not possess a history, none that does not build on or learn from or owe a debt to the work of others. Fame, as we know, accrues to whoever makes the decisive step. Much labour and argument has been expended on the matter of who came first – myself or Mr Edison. I did, ladies and gentlemen, of course, as the record shows – but that is not really the point; neither are the fame or the money. The point was the illumination – the light for people to read and work and think or simply sit companionably by, to drive the darkness outdoors at least.

The means to achieve this, we theorised, was by producing a vacuum in the glass bulb and allowing the filament to heat until it generated light. Why then did this for so long prove to be such a brief candle in practice? As the poet Marvell wrote, you will recall, in his great ode on Cromwell:

Nature that hateth emptiness
Allows of penetration less…

Our problem was that our 'emptiness', our vacuum, was no such thing: the glass chamber was imperfectly purged of atmospheric gas. When I discovered this, I ensured that the vacuum was improved, and the seals around the filaments tightened. But still the bulb would blacken and the light would die.

At length I realised that what I faced was what might be considered an example of 'penetration', of two things occupying the same space – an impossibility, of course – on the one hand the vacuum, on the other the unpurged residues attaching to the filament itself. Until then the instrument of light had tended to produce darkness. But now I saw. And I could account for the processes involved: if the carbon filament were heated to extract the residual gas before being sealed in the bulb, sustained illumination would be achieved. Thus we and our children live in a world of light. Eureka! As the journalists would have us declare.

But the world of light was not the work of a moment, or an accident.

As you also know, what became known as my carbon process enabled the making of photographs of unprecedented quality: the world would not only be illuminated, it would be preserved against the passage of time. This is, of course, the function of art, to preserve, to make, as the poet Horace said, (a monument more lasting than bronze). Immortality, or its image, is what all of us long for, and the image of immortality that I myself have constantly before my mind's eye is a family photograph taken indoors with the benefit of electric light, at the house in Pallion, impossibly. Another case of 'penetration'. It is a crowded picture, for I sit with my two families and my two wives, Fanny and Hannah, all our children and my friend, colleague and brother-in-law John Mawson. The picture is perfect, but as I say, it is impossible.

The disaster which befell us made no sense, I have told myself. It was simply something that must be borne, a part of the pains of the human lot. And of course we are never free of our losses; and why should we wish to be, since they are evidence of the durability of love? Had I seen John Mawson on the day, perhaps at an early meeting in my house at Leazes Terrace, what might we have said?

'Have you everything you require, John?'

'I have my equipment; there will be men to help on the site and to carry the material away to the Town Moor.'

'And is there still no explanation of why the material has been found?'

'None. It was simply discovered in the stable.'

'I feel disquiet at this task you have undertaken, John.'

'Likewise. It is the cost of being both a Chemist and the Sheriff.' We might have laughed at that coincidence. I would not have mentioned that Nobel's own brother Emil had died at twenty-one in an explosion of nitroglycerine at the family's factory in Sweden, or the fatal explosion in San Francisco the previous year. It would not have been necessary to do so.

John and a party of helpers including a police constable and several local youths entered a cellar in Old Swan Yard off Cloth Market where a store of nitroglycerine had been discovered. How it came there and for what intended use seems never to have been satisfactorily determined. The party went by carriage and cart to dispose of the material, John having chosen the Town Moor as an appropriate site. It seems that John and some of his party carried away some of the opened canisters from the place where their liquid contents had been poured away into the earth on the Town Moor, intending to dispose of the remaining crystalline deposits in another spot a little way off. It was then that the disaster occurred. Witnesses said that when the explosion took place the earth shook and that human limbs were seen to be hurled into the air. Now that you have all seen photographs and moving images, you can the better imagine this cruel catastrophe for yourselves: the world is able to turn its attention to its own seeming impossibilities. We can see what cannot and should not be seen.

John Mawson and several others were taken away to hospital, but he died that night of his injuries. My guide and partner, my great encourager, my friend, was snatched away. But this was not all. John Mawson's death seems to have produced what Herr Bodenstein later described as a chain reaction, whereby 'if two molecules react, not only molecules of the final reaction products are formed, but also some unstable molecules, having the property of being able to further react with the parent molecules,' and so on.

Even now I say this as if the impartial language of science might mitigate the subsequent sickness and death of my wife Fanny and then our twin sons, which occurred within a few months of John Mawson's accident. The task of science is to illuminate, is it not? It is possible, though, that there are times when the world it brings into view seems impossible to contemplate, when our sustaining beliefs and the optimism by which I myself had always previously been marked fall away, as into a void without form or meaning. This was my state for a year or more after these several bereavements. My thoughts stagnated and wandered away in a vagrant manner almost without control, and I was left with a painful sense of having neglected to fulfil a duty.

And then we'll shout and shine and sing
And make the Pallion arches ring
When all the Swans come home.

There would be no such homecoming, it seemed.

Later and at different times I wrote the two following sharply contrasting comments in my diary. Firstly: 'the passing of genius through life is like the passing of a shooting star through our atmosphere – coming out of darkness, and quickly re-entering it again; and do what we may, we cannot but repine at this hard law.' Was John Mawson a genius? There was not time even to discover it. But I repined; oh, I did.

Then a little after that I wrote to my second wife, Hannah: 'Thank God for his goodness to us! So far from our deserts.' Is this not also a form of 'penetration', the impossible simultaneous presence of two things – unbearable grief and exalted joy – in the same space? Science seeks to uncover the facts of nature, but what is a fact when the spirit has fled?

After my time of mourning I applied myself once more to my researches until at length (with the aid of steadfast colleagues and German glass-blowers) I succeeded in the task of making an incandescent electric light bulb. In that moment – and I do not say this out of vanity – the world changed. Where hitherto darkness had impatiently awaited its hour, now the light could govern all the hours of the day and night. The light might flicker but it would not fail, you might say. Mechanisms have no sense of irony, of course.

Scientists are often taught to be and often temperamentally inclined to be wary of metaphor: that way magic lies; or poetry. But the human imagination is surely a unity: it can hardly be its own enemy. I immersed myself in poetry from childhood and would quote it throughout my life when the occasion arose. At the death of John Mawson I thought of Milton's 'Lycidas':

> For Lycidas is dead, dead ere his prime:
> Young Lycidas, and hath not left his peer:
> Who would not sing for Lycidas?

And the nature of the scientific events we are able to witness, with their sudden connections and their power to generate new realities, can fairly be viewed as a kind of poetry, just as the poet Coleridge in his great *Biographia Literaria* characterised the poetic imagination as 'a living power and prime agent of all human perception, and…a repetition in the finite mind of the eternal act of creation of the infinite I AM.' It was in this spirit, as part of the God-given process of discovering and forming new unities, that in 1871 I came to seek the hand of Hannah White, Fanny's sister, in marriage. The law of the land was against us, forbidding me to marry my deceased wife's sister, and it would remain so for almost forty years more. But the Swiss order matters differently, and it was to Neuchatel that we travelled to be wed in the eye of God at the Reformed Church in the town. And from this date my happiness began once more, as a result, perhaps, of a chain reaction, in which we could only play our parts in good faith to the best of our ability.

You see what I am doing – making sense, inferring meaning. Meaning, you might say, is not the sphere of the scientist: an observable fact is its own meaning, and its connection to the mind of the creator is not ours to divine. Metaphysics has largely ceased to be part of the empire of science. You might say I am making a category error, or trying to speak one language with the mind of another. Why could I not be happy with electric light and photography and the discovery of artificial fibre? Could they not be enough? Let me affirm that often I was happy, and more than happy, with my second wife and a family to which we added, and with our home, with research and the discovery of items and processes useful to my fellow creatures, with friends and worldly success and the world's applause. But at the edge of things there waited always that realm of restlessness and doubt where it seemed impossible to – to accommodate the spirit to the material nature of things – to glass and metal and filament and vacuum pump and the light that in combination they produced. The light I shed might be only the *image* of the greater light that must, surely, lie behind and beyond all our earthly endeavours; for if that was not so (though it must be so) what was our case, our situation but that of falling through a void, without a solid ground of being?

I was of my time as all men are. I stood for liberal hopefulness, reform, improvement, the harnessing of the productive power of science to the common good. I followed the light faithfully, but could not but be aware of the dark. It may be strange to some that it should be a hymn by John Henry Newman, who was to convert to Catholicism, that seems best to convey these tensions and suggest that faith is continually in the presence of doubt:

> Lead, kindly Light, amid th'encircling gloom, lead Thou
> me on!
> The night is dark, and I am far from home; lead Thou
> me on!
> Keep Thou my feet; I do not ask to see
> The distant scene; one step enough for me.
> So long Thy power hath blest me, sure it still will lead
> me on.
> O'er moor and fen, o'er crag and torrent, till the night
> is gone,
> And with the morn those angel faces smile, which I
> Have loved long since, and lost awhile!
> Meantime, along the narrow rugged path, Thyself hast
> trod,
> Lead, Saviour, lead me home in childlike faith, home to
> my God.
> To rest forever after earthly strife
> In the calm light of everlasting life.

May it be so. I have come to doubt it, but I cannot abandon the possibility, and I know that to some that might make me the less a scientist. All I can do is admit to my ever-present questioning. I was a Victorian optimist, as I have said. I survived terrible loss. I hope I have been of help to others. Yet I speak now in the New Year of 1914, when it is clear to all serious observers that Europe is on the threshold of a great and terrible conflict which may bring the world we know wholly to destruction. How can it be that Christendom permits and even nurtures such a menace to humanity? Can it be that the great imaginative energies of science and industry have brought us into the light only that we may see the better to kill one another before plunging back into the darkness, like so many spent Lucifers into the ruined cities of hell?

Put on the lights in any case. I have no answer, and perhaps you are laughing at me, a man without irony or cynicism or knowingness to help him on his way. But in the teeth of the present evidence I end with an affirmation by a poet who himself knew doubt on intimate terms.

> that which we are, we are;
> One equal temper of heroic hearts,
> Made weak by time and fate, but strong in will
> To strive, to seek, to find, and not to yield.

I say again: put on the lights. What else can we do, after all? Good night.

Certain Measures

'God's a super-director.
He's terribly good at crowd scenes.'
– Peter Porter

THE WHITE TRANSIT HAD been parked normally at the Oxford Street end of Soho Square from 6am. Its index number would warn off traffic wardens. At the same time to the north there were roadworks in readiness in Rathbone Street and a burst water-main being created on Hanway Street, with similar arrangements in place on all exits in the immediate area. Access at the junction with Charing Cross Road and Tottenham Court Road was already bottlenecked by the never-ending re-building of the Underground. The weather was wet and the day was never to become fully light. Final briefings took place at 8am. and the teams dispersed to their positions.

I came down the cut past the Pillars of Hercules and paused in the Square where the beggars were waiting by the railings under the leafless trees. It was London, unmistakeably. The second vehicle, dark blue, was a hundred yards away, empty at present.

I banged on the side door of the white van. It slid open and I climbed in. It was just to keep the watchers on their toes. The watchers were always eating, as if their silent confinement brought a danger of starvation which only bacon rolls and pizzas and vile childish sugary drinks could prevent. But they would eat and watch at the same time, which was something. The screens were showing examples of a rather sodden ordinariness, with staff arriving at the department stores, taxis and white vans much like this one impatiently nosing along, their drivers shouting into their headphones. Underfoot the discarded free-sheets were already turning to mush. The watchers, young ex-soldiers with shaved heads and few opinions, were as absorbed in their work as they were in the console games that occupied their free hours.

I climbed out of the van and set off for a look around. You have to walk the ground, in case. Despite the poor weather and the continuing economic crisis, the area was busy as soon as the shops began to open. Christmas was upon us. There was a slightly reckless atmosphere among the crowds as if being short of funds was in itself a kind of permission or invitation, or incitement, to spend. Oxford Street: the centre of the universe construed as a shoddy brick-and-marble canyon denatured by the self-consuming commercial imperative that our lifetime has brought to perfection. A grimy hole. A major selection of real estate. Invisible in its familiarity. There is nothing to see, ladies and gentlemen. Move along, please.

As I made my way along and around and inside all this for the umpteenth time, spending the hours slowly, wondering what factor might have gone unconsidered by the planners immured in their cave of numbers, it was, as always, interesting to witness that seasonally intensified combination of liberty and fatalism. The bright-faced resentful wives making the best of things – can they have supposed it would come to this? They who had been desired at squash clubs and swimming pools? And the Chinese students ignoring the whites and waving the big stick of *remnin*: what satisfaction could such an easy conquest afford? Or the girls from other shops and offices let loose with their plastic in the dim noontide of the last shopping day before Christmas: what are we to make of them? What are they for, these screeching twos and threes crammed into the dark grubby dim-lit pubs behind the shops, chasing vodka with vodka, comparing their purchases in ever-higher registers of incredulous and unconvincing delight?

They were all, it had been generally accepted, ends in themselves, though it would surprise them were you to put it to them that way, in the unlikely event of your ending up in conversation in a crammed bar, in that sea of fleeting sexual possibility. A grim husband or two, late as usual, stood sinking doubles, their hopeless treasures crammed between their feet. The poor, with no business here, trudged along as though given a different and mistaken map. Distraction sought distraction from itself. Some of these people were us, of course, though we never acknowledged each other.

The waves of shoppers formed and broke, narrowing for the escalators in the bigger stores, jostling on the slick steps of Tottenham Court Road Underground, with rain in their hair, with other people's breath and sheer damp bodily pressure too much with them for comfort or good humour. It was what happened instead of life, which was elsewhere or late or unfairly denied them. The clock ticked on.

With an hour to kill, I took myself to Foyles. Disliking the seasonal crush of blunderers on the lower floors, at first I was unable to settle, but after a time I found an unvisited corner and re-read Kleist's essay 'On the Puppet Theatre'. I realised that I had misunderstood it all those years ago, disfiguring it with my own assumptions. The dance of the marionettes for the entertainment of the common people, observed by Kleist and his companion, a noted professional dancer, there and then in 1810 on the streets of M– (Mainz? Metz?), is more natural than anything the human practitioner of dance can achieve. The marionette is untroubled by gravity as by the habit of reflection that, since the Fall, has separated us from the world. To regain grace we must travel to the ends of the earth and find a new entry to Paradise. How could I have misunderstood? People are not automata, though to gain salvation they must become so.

I peered down the stairwell at the Christmas crowd. Morlocks. When the lost grace returns, the dancer concludes, 'it will be most purely present in the human frame that has either no consciousness or an infinite amount of it, which is to say either in a marionette or in a god.' There would only be a few gods, it seemed to me.

Next I sought out the theology section and a selection of the sermons of Cardinal Newman. The book fell open as though I had marked the passage:

> If Scripture is to be our guide, it is quite plain that the most conscientious, religious, high-principled, honourable men…may be on the side of evil, may be Satan's instruments in cursing, if that were possible, and at least in seducing and enfeebling the people of God.

There it was, as ever, on its barely-consulted shelf, lost like a treasure-ship in a deep ocean trench; a statement both true and impotent to counter what it proposed. How apt to read it at the very hour when the President knelt in prayer at Cathedral.

The rain had a reliable, immiserating steadiness as I finally crossed Charing Cross Road, and made my way up to the monitoring centre. The citizens looked down, not up. They responded to each other with a combination of irritation and mistrust. But they didn't go home, they didn't cut their losses. It was growing dark and still more of them arrived, as if following a summons. They were doing their economic duty: credit where it's due.

I was in my seat in the observation room in good time. Heads turn expectantly among the rows on screens.

At four-thirty the signal went out. The side streets to the north were discreetly and convincingly blocked. At the exit to Soho Square the two white vans collided and an ambulance approached from the direction of Greek Street. As the smoke and teargas canisters rained down from the roofs, a double police line in riot gear, their ID numbers removed, emerged from Berwick Street. People to the west were pointed back to the junction with Regent Street, and those to the east towards the bottleneck at Tottenham Court Road Underground where the traffic lights had just ceased to work and traffic was at a furious standstill. Fifty covert officers in plain clothes had been seeded in the crowd here, fresh from acting as rioters on a specially built reproduction of this location at the Civil Order Training School near Devizes. Uniformed police now blocked the pedestrian exit from Oxford Street. There had been an incident, people were told. Keep calm and co-operate and walk that way in an orderly fashion.

Surely, you might think, the outcome simply could not be predicted. There was nothing inevitable here. I can quite see why it is necessary to think so. But you would be wrong. This event had been exhaustively gamed. On the banks of screens in the monitoring centre, the crowd in the zone thickened, coughing and half-blind from the gas, herded along by the steadily advancing police line behind them. The shops were hastily locking their doors while the customers inside peered out at the street, many showing that odd resentment that accompanies incomprehension. It was typical, some of them would certainly be saying. More smoke and gas rained down. There were the beginnings of panic.

When the crowd – two thousand plus – was confined in a space a hundred and fifty yards deep and as wide as the street, the plainclothes element went into violent action against those at the front, driving the mass back on itself and in turn bringing the rear of the crowd into collision with the uniformed police line, who responded in kind.

We kept the sound off. Now there was panic. The crowd-mind turned on itself as we had known it would. Fractious families were separated. People fell underfoot, 'for pavement to the abject rear', as the poet has it. Even in the crush some people stole from one another. The solidarity displayed was of an impacted, physical kind. People suffocated, crushed against lamp-posts and plate-glass windows while those inside looked on at this unprecedented performance.

Yet it was not unprecedented: Ibrox, Hillsborough, Burnden Park, the Poll Tax and Occupy disorders, the Love Parade – all of these were an education, the inferences refined to an exactitude that might be taken for supernatural. This crowd in this place at this time and under these conditions meets with these intensifying constraints and, with a little help, sets about destroying itself. We had done our sums.

The media couldn't get near the place. The CCTV had been, they were told, knocked out by some means. Afterwards those able to leave the area had phones and other devices confiscated, while the dead and injured were stripped of their possessions. It was a terrorist incident, clearly. Everyone was a suspect until told otherwise

On the six o'clock news the Commissioner of the Metropolitan Police explained that an investigation on an unexpected scale was under way and that arrests were already being made.

The Prime Minister addressed the nation at nine o'clock about the Emergency Public Order regulations she was now regretfully compelled to put into effect. Her remarks were preceded by our own footage of the Oxford Street incident, showing the anarchists' unprovoked attacks on innocent public going about its festive business in the days before what was, lest we forget, a religious festival enshrined in the hearts of the nation. Democracy had to set limits, she said, or risk being drowned in a tide of terrorist bloodshed. Enough was enough, and for the greater good the right of public assembly would become, for a time, discretionary. Those who might object to this, most immediately the organisers and intending participants in a large welfare rights protest planned for New Year, should consider the responsibilities of citizenship and remove their tanks from the nation's lawn. No protest would now be permitted, for reasons evident to all reasonable decent people. I wondered who wrote her material.

In the street below, as the smoke dispersed, were shoes and hats and chainstore bags. About a hundred injured and a dozen dead. It was enough to tip the balance. The faces at the monitors were grey with anti-climax. I told them to go, but to avoid Soho that evening. Left to myself I began to write up my notes, while looking again at some of the footage. Anyone who saw this – and there'd be very few of them – would be tempted to say it looked like another country, and – had they been looking – had been so for a long time. Another England, in almost every detail resembling the place where they thought they lived, to the extent that these faithful consumers thought at all. I could remember the old place. Shame it couldn't last. It seemed long ago. So too by the time I'd finished writing, did the afternoon's events. I would prepare a formal draft of the report the following day.

I took another look at one sequence: I know her, I thought, that fair-haired young woman in the pale raincoat, pinned against the outside of a telephone box as the crush swayed and thickened. She was struggling to do something. Of course: to get her mobile phone out. She couldn't know that the signals were blocked for that hour in the West End. She stared at the phone as if it might come suddenly to life and then raised it over her head. She was trying to photograph what she could see. A hand reached up and took the phone away, and as she turned to protest someone not seen struck her a blow from behind. A momentary gap opened in the startled crowd and she fell into it and disappeared as the mass reformed over her. I know her, I thought. I knew her, the daughter of a colleague with whose wife I had an affair twenty years before. I declined to draw the sentimental inference. There was nothing to be done.

I closed the room and went down to the street. It was deserted, as for the most part was Soho, and I walked for a long time until I found a pub. It was a little subdued, perhaps, but people were in there making the best of things or not noticing things. A group of young women sat together. The news was on and they watched it with the conspicuous attention of people who want to be thought of responsible adult citizens but are secretly (they suppose) a bit bored. One by one they turned to their phones. One of them saw me looking. Her expression became sarcastic. What was *I* looking at? I gave the slightest shake of my head, glanced up at the screen for a moment, looked back and continued to stare at her. She had the sense to look away. The fact is, everybody knows, really. Of course they do, gods, puppets and high-minded evildoers such as me. As the Scots say, we know fine.

Lovely

THE MOMENT YOU STEP on to the evening Metro you are free, you tell yourself. You have no address, no occupation, no demeaning acquaintances or family ties, no history. You are born out of nothing. The world lies all before you, issuing its invitation to the voyage on this blue evening. Who needs the beautiful convex ceilings of the Paris Metro, when you have this near-empty train running through scattered settlements and scrub fields towards the sea-coast of your desires?

Sitting at the front of the train, you pour a very little more into the space between thumb and forefinger. It burns cold as it travels into the brain, scouring away the layers of habit and disappointment as it goes. There is no yesterday.

The train stops here and there. People wander off into their limitations, their little rooms where the dead light flickers on the screens. Let them. Liberty is not for everyone. You lean into the long coastward curve, dreaming an ecstasy of destinations. It feels as if you are crossing a continent, the alleys of hawthorn and the stone bridges touched by your stylish, patient urgency.

The evening sea wheels into view, with a vessel out on the horizon like a promise. The world is elsewhere, you were always taught, so take what you are given. But no more of that, the old dispensation. No more.

A final bridge and you are slowing, as if the train answers to your desire alone. At the near end of the platform the refurbishments continue, the slim iron pillars stripped back to rust, their winged, floral tops half-repainted in the green–gold colours of summer, while the canopy slowly grows back over the platform to complete the pattern once again. All this is done as if in honour of your arrival here this evening, suave libertine and ladykiller. The doors open. You step out and see the opened concourse gate, and watch as the other travellers melt away about their business. And for a moment you are afraid.

For a moment you pause, uncertain where to turn. The station waits with you, its signs and warnings like discreetly raised eyebrows. It is not too late to cross the bridge and take the next train back. But the thought of your room is terrible, a pauper's grave for desire and imagination. Courage!

But surely this is not the kind of place where it happens. It is at once too obvious and too unlikely. People think of it as theirs, even if it's years since they've actually been here (to the market on Sunday, perhaps, looking for books or curiosities). Perhaps they haven't even been through on the Metro for a while, but they still have a sense of ownership and that weird kind of mutual dependence that can make some people weep at the idea of a Co-op being pulled down or a sports ground turned into a car park for lawyers and accountants.

So this is not the kind of place where it happens. The topless iron pillars and their rusty flowers, out on the fenced-off bits of the platforms, indicate this, and so do the wooden planks on the floor of the covered bridge – the bridge whose upward curve lifts the heart as though at homecoming. The vast, peaceable spaces of the concourse under the mild grey light of the glass-panelled roof say so too: not here. Try one of the others, one of the out-of-the-way stations along the river, where nobody seems to get on or off. Or even go south of the river, if it means that much. But look where you may, you will find no place as beautiful. And where else is there a station which also offers a gallery and exhibition space?

On the blind side of the foot of the double stairs of the

bridge you top yourself up. And then, somehow, here you are, in the restaurant, thinking tonight might be the night. There is spring in the air, that sense of a stream suddenly running again at the back of the air after being sealed underground for months on end. People are drawn out into the unaccustomed light, as if beginning to remember that life is possible. And somehow here she is, across the table, real in every particular and laughing at one of your jokes in a perfectly natural way that you find almost unbearably exciting. It is all too real to be possible. She raises her glass to toast your wit. But when did she arrive?

Nothing of that kind has ever happened before. If it were not such a beautiful, newly-wakened April evening, with the trains coming and going lightly on the breeze, carrying their vast suggestions of elsewhere, inviting you to board here and now for the voyage; and if she were not so darkly beautiful and unplaceably adult in years, and despite her laughter, serious, serious, you might think this was a cruel joke at your expense. It would not be the first delusion that spring has encouraged you to indulge. Your history is bitter with deceptions. But not tonight. Tonight, you are sure, that is not the case. Things must be as they seem.

And on the mundane level she has already said that you will both have to pay, because that is only fair at a first meeting. Both of you will have to pay. She smiled on saying this, as though something was being understood – for example, that to speak of a first meeting implies others, and that already she would be well-disposed towards the prospect of further occasions like this. You are happy to go along with the idea, to swim in the wine-warm current of the evening as if all the evenings will be like this, as if it must be the case that there will be other evenings for you and her, more hours in mild lamplight, more delicate negotiations in which the menu serves as a token of possibly erotic good faith.

You are both carnivores: that too is a sign. Oysters with Chablis, steak with a heavyweight Medoc, sorbet, coffee, the bitterest chocolate, grappa for the heroic close: the heavy card of the menu stretches downward before you into the deepening blue of the evening. Eat, she says. It's rude to stare. But she doesn't mind. You slowly eat your haemorrhaging steaks and let the peppery, dream-heavy wine sit in the laps of your tongues.

How much have you drunk? You seem to think this is the third bottle of red, and that she has been ordering the new ones, which is unusual, and yet you feel not so much drunk as magnified, intensified in your person, as though reaching a potential which has hitherto seemed more of an aspiration than a certainty. All the other days have been the journey to this day, to this triumphant station of the night. You are happy to drink: you imagine your white shirt turning slowly raspberry-crimson, a slow smooth wave sinking from the neck. And this arouses you.

She too raises her glass as you do, but it is as though the wine merely brushes her lips (and yet her glass empties as yours does). The wine brushes the carmine lipstick in the pale, Slavic face where her green eyes flash with wit and recognition and suggestion and perhaps with invitation, of the kind exchanged without words between people of the world, urbane spirits such as you and her, as though in fact you must be equals.

The only pity is how many years it has taken to arrive at this, this station of the night (you like that phrase), how many wasted nights, disappointments, deceptions, humiliations, stopped-clock solitudes, agonised appraisals in the grey of the shaving mirror at dawn. You were made for better things, for your companion in black, her lipstick and her flashing gaze of promise, made for this night-platform and the ecstasy its destination promises.

No need, no need to disturb this seeming equilibrium as you carve your steaks with a slight amusing sense of déjà vu, and consume them and follow with strawberries and more wine and then a strange green-tinged vodka you have never come across before but which the waiter brings almost before she requests it. The spirit burns and cleans and clarifies the palate as though now it will be ready for anything, and the stream of jokes and anecdotes and charm and hints of hints continues to flow both ways between you, like a paradox it would be vulgar to refer to. It is, you suppose, a little like being a god, supposing such creatures existed – those with world enough and time to summon all Creation to their steady gaze. It is almost like a competition, you think, but dismiss the idea, raising a clean glass in honour of this crimson night.

When did it grow dark? When were the candles brought to the table, and when did the discerning handful of other customers leave? You feel the hunger once again, provoking the wine to new heights of ardour.

She explains that she did not use her real name in arranging this meeting. You reciprocate. You laugh together. She says you cannot be too careful. After all, there are a lot of lunatics out there. *And what about in here*, you think, but do not say aloud, or rather, hope you have not said aloud – for by this stage of elevation the interior and exterior are hard to separate. The self is shrugging off its bonds to move into the sphere of pure becoming. This is what you always had in mind. This is what all those others were the preparation for, for such a night as this, the thirsty self's apotheosis. You wish that both of you could live forever. Oh, if that were possible.

Now, with no transition, you are out on the station concourse. How did you leave the restaurant? She smiles in the muted light as though she knows what you are thinking and enjoys your surprise, as though she had a hand in its preparation in order to enjoy your bemused delight as the pair of you move like dancers over the flagstones towards the wrought-iron platform gate but then up the stairs on to the curving bridge. She has taken off her shoes and moves in stockinged feet like a dancer. Has she no coat?

All the years and all the others seem far off now, like momentary elements in the life of someone else, rehearsals for the real thing. All the reflection and planning, the visualisation, the contrivance, were only servants of this supreme occasion. You feel as if you might leave the ground, losing contact with the earth and earthly things, with history, with the life you have led until now. You could weep, for this, you fear, is perfection: beyond this there is nowhere left to go. Beyond this lie merely the ashes of ordinary mortality. She understands: her glance assures you.

You ascend the bridge and as you pass the glassed-in exhibition space she places a hand on your arm to stop you. *Look*, she gestures, then places a finger to her lips. The long gallery is full of dancers, couples turning slowly to a silent music. They wear the evening costume of a far-off decade, and you feel underdressed in comparison. What is her point? She produces a key and inserts it in the discreet door and you slip through on to the dancefloor.

The space smells heavy with musky perfume. The dancers revolve, intent on each other and the music. She leads you to the middle of the wooden floor, to a space in the silent crowd. From nowhere she has poured a few grains on her hand and offers it to you, then takes some for herself. She indicates that you, the man, must lead. As you place a hand on her bare back and take her cold hand in yours, you begin to hear the music, though hearing is not the sense involved – or rather, you can hear with all your senses, this music both new and very ancient whose power teaches you the steps in an instant.

Almost too much, almost too much, you think, as you master an elegant turn – at the same moment as you see that the male figures around you have all had their throats cut, the white shirts turned to sheets of blood, the blood running down the curved floor, while their partners, who have no faces, urge them firmly on in the pattern of the dance. You understand that everything you see is true. You feel the neat blade slip from ear to ear. You see your partner stand above you, her gaze grave in its appraisal, before she stoops to put her shoes back on. You hear her footsteps, the locking of the door, then fainter footsteps. For a little while you wake again, and what you hear is the sound of the last Metro pulling away from the station into the night, and what you see is the reflection of its lights on the ceiling of the gallery, while the shadowy dancers continue to turn.

III

Quartier Perdu

Dear Susan,

I'm sorry not to have written sooner. It has all been a rush, the journey, arrival, moving in, half-unpacking, and wondering what I have let myself in for. So this is really my first chance to sit down and try – well, to think, I suppose. There was already a letter awaiting me from Chicago – Aunt Mercy determined to keep a hold on her wandering niece. She thinks scholarship will make a spinster of me. But it's to you that I'm writing first before beginning to properly unpack, as I sit down at my table at the end of the Atlantic sea-crossing and the smoky, shuffling charm of the train from Boulogne. Now I can look about me for a minute or two. The annoying fact is that my large steamer-trunk has failed to arrive, and I must for the moment make do with the clothes in my suitcase. I foresee expenditure! Not something to tell Aunt Mercy.

The fact that you'll join me in Paris in the spring gives me the courage to face what I've taken on by agreeing to come to this place first! It is by no means Paris, though some Symbolist and Decadents professed to prefer it. With its air of long-established decline and time suspended, I can quite see why they made that claim. I'm not immune either, though I think it unlikely I shall be besotted by the time we meet. Why did I choose August Hendrik for my poet? No need to remind me. He was a field where I would have few rivals, an undiscovered country. I have made my bed, as Aunt Mercy would no doubt be quick to say. There is too much to do. I quail at the scope of the task – and after that to write it up and face the doctoral committee. I must have courage. Send me some of yours!

Vlaaminck Straat, on the eastern edge of the city, is a neglected street with no commercial premises. The city itself is quite depopulated – quite as I imagined from reading the supremely gloomy Rodenbach – spires, grey canals, high-walled secret gardens, narrow streets that sidle away on business they do not care to disclose. And bells at all hours flustering the swans that sleep in the shelter of the bridges now autumn and its fog and rain are here. It is all romantic in a damp, dank, underheated, European way.

I have an attic room that looks over the red-grey roofs to the vast and gloomy cathedral, and hidden away in those streets is the whole sense of teeming, secret life that any bookish person, or person of imagination, will find irresistibly suggestive. When I return to take my doctorate and marry Randall (see how firmly I state that intention, and I should write to him when I finish this), my travelling days are likely to be over. That is the bargain. I shall be a wife in Milwaukee, married to a Milwaukee lawyer. So I must make the most of this season of liberty!

As to the object of my journey, the papers of the poet Hendrik, well, here they are, bursting from drawers and cupboards and filling any available surface. It is an unholy mess. The plan, as I told you, is that when all is set in order the house will become a place of pilgrimage and study. Who will come? None that I can see.

For all the bells, in the house itself it is very quiet. It feels as if everything has already happened, or has at any rate been decided. Such an atmosphere!

Now I must go and take tea with the Ickxes. I'll tell you about them in my next. Remember me to your mother.

Much love,

Joanna

19 Vlaaminck Straat
27th September 1932

Dear Susan,

Here I am in the Lost Quarter! That is what the local people – I mean the Ickxes, the housekeepers here – call this district. Its name suits it very well, for even in a city where little happens and few appear to live and almost no one to work, Vlaaminck Straat and its neighbourhood seem as though under a spell of silence and emptiness – the ever-ringing bells notwithstanding. If I need to go to the stores I must walk along the grey web of canals, seeing only a few stooped widows and almost never a child, into the centre of the Old City, where there is a market most days and a few old-established emporia where I could buy enough lace to stuff a hope chest ten times over, but scarcely a thing for anyone younger than Aunt Mercy to wear, while books and newspapers in English are not to be found at any price! The works of Hendrik and his contemporaries can be had in beautiful editions, but no one seems to buy them. Every square has a bust of its revered and ignored poet, though I have yet to find Hendrik's monument.

It is a little lonely, but of course I have plenty to occupy me in the house, where I'm beginning to understand the scale of my task. Half a year is nothing. A year cannot be enough. Five would be too short. But of course I don't tell the Ickxes that. I must make the best of it.

I must try to describe the Ickxes for you. They are brother and sister, Anselm and Gertrud, dark and pale, six feet tall, skinny as rakes, of an age impossible to determine. Mme Ickx is, well, Victorian; tightly corseted in floor-length black with a lace collar and cuffs. Her brother wears an ancient black high-collared suit. I thought they might be in costume to enhance the effect of the place, but no, they mean it. They are, I gather, descendants of the couple who kept house for Hendrik, although it is hard to imagine them actually being born. They seem permanent and unchanging, like the heavy black furniture that looms about the place. They are here to greet the visitors, who do not come, and to show them round the old apartments, Hendrik's study and so on. They are retainers with no one to retain, giving off an implacable fidelity. You will infer that I do not like them, but I do not think liking is the point with the Ickxes. They are not as other people but belong instead in an old children's book as an example of something sinister and unwholesome. In fact, they are like very old children. They are unfailingly polite, but in such a way as to suggest they are reading from a card of instructions.

They seem wholly un-bookish – I have not seen inside their rooms, which are in the basement and I imagine as being semi-submerged, for the Ickxes are damp – but they know enough to guide my initial foray into the vast accumulation of letters and manuscripts of which my archival task is composed. Also they watch me. If one is not there, the other is in the offing, bringing thick black coffee and little plates of chocolate, coming in and going out like the couple in a cathedral clock, though of course they are not married but brother and sister. The house, of course, has no actual children. Wherever they go a sweet, heavy smell follows as though disguising another less tolerable odour. As you see, I have fallen into a storybook!

I must go now. Next time I will tell you about the Markgraf. Perhaps our letters will cross. Yours may have been delayed somehow.

With love,

Joanna

Vlaaminck Straat

5th October 1932

Dearest Susan,

I think there may be something wrong with the mails. Otherwise nothing would prevent a steady bombardment of helpful and suspicious advice from Aunt Mercy. And I have nothing from you or Randall. Or have you all decided to dislike me and abandon me?

I have been ill – some kind of fever that confined me to bed for a few days, which meant being waited on by Mme Ickx, with watery soup that I am sure she ladles out of the canal, and the usual chokingly thick and oversweet coffee which she insists is a panacea. Part of the time I was in a kind of delirium where there was a good deal of coming and going, doors opening and closing, heavy bunches of keys, voices cut off, words not quite audible.

The amphibian Mme Ickx is evidently immune to what has ailed me. She tells me it is a sickness specific to the region, one that comes every autumn and carries off children. I am hard put to believe there are any children in this dank grey town. It is all widows and their sons, or else the Ickxes, neither of whom can be imagined as breeding. What need of more of them when they already exist?

When I felt able to get up, I made to go downstairs to place a letter to Aunt Mercy in the hall for posting. Mme Ickx insisted that it was too soon for me to risk the stairs and that she would deal with the letter. In her blank, watery way she is very kind, though as ever a little too much present. So anyway, I sat in my room and read Hendrik's long correspondence about grimoires with that old fraud Eliphas Levi. By next day I was recovered and insisted on getting back to work filing the mountain of letters. So far I have reached 1895 – Hendrik frequently ill and looking beyond this world yet assiduous in his dealings with his bankers – there was a lot of money here, and who knows where it can have gone? All this takes time, of course, and there is still a good deal of mountain to be moved. After the letters come manuscripts, diaries, contracts.

I remember that I said I would tell you about the Markgraf, but now I come to do so it's hard to say anything definite about him. The Ickxes have begun to speak of him in the last day or two. He is not here but he is expected. He has been a long time away. It seems unclear when he will arrive or how indeed the Ickxes know that he will, but they give a sense of careful preparation. They have laid fires – very welcome – in the library and my attic, which Anselm Ickx tends with gloomy care. I do not quite like having him be near my things when I am not present, but to object would surely seem discourteous.

The Ickxes do not respond to questions about the Markgraf, but he recurs in their speech as one having a proverbial or legendary status – what the Markgraf would do or say, signs of his approach in the deepening of the season and the flight of birds – I'm making the last part up, or at least I think I am! The Markgraf is associated in the minds of the Ickxes with somewhere they call The Old House (they say it as though with reverent initial capitals), which is not the same as this house but seems close at hand, though like the Markgraf it is oddly unspecific.

So we await the Markgraf! There are no pictures of him.

When I asked Anselm Ickx why this should be, he seemed baffled at the idea that there might be such things. There are pictures of Hendrik, though, looking consumptive and boring, glooming about by the side of various canals, or standing pensively in graveyards.

I am still – can you tell? – drowsy with the dregs of the fever, over-warm and yet anxious and wrought-up somehow, and, though I can work an hour or two downstairs, I lack the energy, and perhaps, I fear, even the confidence to go out into the town at present. I am sure that all it will require is a letter from home to stir me. There is no telephone, and when I mentioned telegrams the Ickxes professed themselves unable to grasp the idea. Since I have no reason to panic, this need not matter. How I long for an American newspaper!

So here I am, in the Lost Quarter, a little lost and homesick for far-off Chicago and longing for your news.

All love,

Joanna

29 Vlaaminck Straat

21st October 1932

Dearest Susan,

No post at all. Not from you, nor Aunt Mercy, nor Randall. Not a word. Is no one curious? Strange. Home has come to seem very distant from these dim rooms and the watery crepuscular light of this town with its air of perpetual valediction. I have found myself wondering if there is any purpose served in continuing to write when, for whatever reason, there is no reply. But it is a discipline and a clarifying habit, and so I shall continue. It puts the labours among Hendrik's absurd papers in a saner perspective.

The sickness recurs intermittently, as I have heard is also

the case with malaria. For a day, or two days, I have had to take to my bed before resuming the Sisyphean task. Hendrik was not a good poet. I think I always knew that. For a professed Satanist he seems curiously lacking in vital energy. When he was not imagining himself trafficking with the underworld he was usually prostrated with an unspecified malaise that sounds rather like my own. To that extent I can sympathise.

The most interesting thing about him is his correspondence with the artist and caricaturist Felicien Rops. Rops has a real whiff of sulphur about him. When Hendrik describes an interview with the Devil, Rops merely asks Hendrik for precise visual details. What, for example, was the Devil wearing? A morning coat? A smoking jacket? Hendrik entirely fails to grasp the tone of these enquiries. Rops was confident that if the Devil should manifest himself anywhere in Flanders it would be to Rops in Namur and certainly not to Hendrik hereabouts. Hendrik confided that he had made a pact with the Devil in exchange for literary immortality. I think he was robbed. Rops sent him a sketch of a moustachioed gentleman looking rather like Joseph Conrad, neatly besuited and with a smart cane, seated across the roaring fireplace from a donkey likewise suited and seated. At last Hendrik seems to have understood Rops's attitude, for the correspondence ends there. All very foolish and day-before-yesterday dusty and dim. I have made a foolish choice, but how can I give up now?

Now I have to sleep, though it is scarcely afternoon. As autumn deepens and grows chill under these leaden skies and whistling chimney-pots I fancy it is growing hard to tell day from night.

Do write to me.

Yours ever,

Joanna

29 Vlaaminck Straat
5th November

Do you think it is possible to lose days, weeks even, by somehow being distracted, by not paying attention, by losing the power of attention, losing even oneself somehow? There is a space in my mind into which some days have vanished; a lost quarter of my own that I cannot quite come at, where time should be. I remember working, cataloguing a number of unpublished poems, then feeling sick once more, and going in miserable frustration to bed and being ministered to by Mme Ickx, but I cannot picture the days or establish the duration of this fugue-like passage. But there is an episode, a real event, I am sure of it, that remains clear in the murk.

I had gone down into the garden. It seems a long time since I had the energy or the nerve to go out into the town – I suspect I would not be able to find my way about now – but perhaps I thought it would do me good to take some fresh air in the garden. There is some nagging problem with my sight, a discontinuous interruption by spectral grids and barricades of the kind associated with migraine. For some reason I was wearing my nightgown and a wrapper – oh yes, Mme Ickx explained that my other clothes must be boiled to prevent infection. First I looked at the mossy statue of a faun crouched with his pipe on a brick plinth among old cypresses. Then I went and stood at the gate in the wall at the end of the garden, looking into the still canal that curved away on either hand, and across at the burnt-orange brick of the houses opposite, their windows shuttered as if that district had been closed up indefinitely, as if a plague had driven the residents out of town. I thought how easy it would be simply to dissolve, like ash into the grey water and have done with it all – all this hopeless work, these bad poems and foolish letters and diaries full of childish incantations. This infection, you see, is very literary. Be done with scholarship, with home, with Randall – and at this point I realised that I could no longer picture Randall's face.

I turned to go indoors, thinking I must see the photograph I kept in my diary. A movement made me look up – not at the windows of number 29, but at the house next door, where, at an attic window adjacent to my own, the dead white face of Mme Ickx stared down at me. She held my gaze a few moments, then turned and spoke to someone I could not see, and moved out of sight.

How I came to wake up back in bed I cannot remember. Mme Ickx was leaning over me to wipe my face with a damp cloth. In the background her brother stood silently.

I must have a doctor, I said. And she replied, There are no doctors, Mademoiselle, not for this complaint. I asked if I would die. She told her brother to run a bath. Again I asked if would die. She stroked my forehead and replied: It is not yet your time, Mademoiselle. Have courage. What were you doing next door? I asked. I do not understand, she replied. And her brother said, No one is next door.

She helped me from the bed into the bathroom, where she washed me like a child, singing as to a child. Then there is another gap, until now.

I feel I shall forget my name. Send someone to look for me. I cannot find my clothes.

21st November

Time dissolves, it seems to me. I know what the calendar in the library says. I have seen Anselm Ickx dutifully turning the cog for a new day. But time dissolves, and I dissolve in what is left – this grey, wintry air that seeps around the casements and along the corridors. If life were over it would feel this way.

I am not writing this to anyone – or to myself, maybe,

whoever I used to be, the one that names escape, including her own. I write propped up in bed like some doomed nineteenth-century heroine, lost high up beneath the whistling tiles, wearing a damp grey nightdress, high at the neck and buttoned at the wrists, produced by Mme Ickx. My beautiful peach and ivory things have not been given back. The regimen is coffee like sugared glue, followed by canal soup, and Mme Ickx watches me drinking what she brings, and her brother stands blankly in the door of my room as if for long periods he can simply cease to be, a pale golem who has wandered off the shelf and into the world, if that is what this place is.

The Markgraf is coming.

I got out again yesterday (I think). Down for a breath of air in the garden, sweating with fever despite the cold, wearing hardly a stitch, as Mme Ickx later reprovingly observed. The faun was still there, still silently piping, his expression now seeming one of repellent glee. I had almost no strength but made myself go to the wall at the end of the garden. The canal was as before, empty and unmoving.

The Markgraf is coming. You whom I have lost, who have forgotten me, can you not hear him? Can you not hear the seething quiet of his progress?

I sat down on a bench. I tried not to turn and look at the houses, but my gaze was helplessly drawn to the attic window of the house next door. And there I stood, looking back at me, naked but for a necklace of rubies, and the pearls woven into my piled hair.

Once again I awoke in this room, in this bed, with Mme Ickx's sick sweetness to watch over me. The house is awake now. The Markgraf is coming. And now, next door, The Old House listens too, in a clenched silence of anticipation. August Hendrik was no poet. He was something else, in return for which the Markgraf is coming to claim his due.

I awoke again in the blue-grey dusk. The house is in the grip of intense heat, as if afire downstairs. I dragged myself to the window and looked out. I have travelled somehow, into The Old House. The faun stepped down from his plinth and went clip-clopping to the water-gate, as though to greet an arrival. Anselm and Gertrud Ickx followed after. And then there came silently into view a splendid black sailing-barge with sails of a sickly, sulphurous yellow. It moored at the gate. The Markgraf is coming. Soon his footsteps will ascend and he will enter and find me, here in The Old House, as was intended. If anyone who knows or cares for me should ever read this final page, then be assured: the room where I am sealed is very close, the merest step away, and inside it will be pits and chains, fires, abysses, orgies, eternities and screams without end. Whatever you do, never open the door.

Keeping Count

PATRICK DUVEEN HAD ARRANGED his own transport across the Lagoon. He didn't want to travel on the waterbus from Fondamente Novo with Stella Slattery and the rest. That would be like a pensioners' outing, with the ashes in the urn inside a bag like a packed lunch. Instead, the hired water-taxi had come to his hotel, the wordless boatman leaving him to his thoughts as they wove their way towards the Canale Della Misericordia and then out into the Lagoon, which took 150 seconds. The cemetery island lay waiting in the sunlight of the chill October noontide, rich, exact and otherworldly, as if extracted from a test-piece for Böcklin's *The Isle of the Dead* – cypresses, the high obscuring wall, the roofs of the mausolea. 75 seconds to make the crossing.

The view was satisfactory as always, but Duveen resented it being wasted on the interment of Benedict Slattery's ashes. It was an affectation on Slattery's part, or on Stella, his widow's. Stella was an actress, of sorts, so of course the thing had to be staged. Slattery had no particular connection with Venice. Was there something wrong with the North London Necropolis that they had to come all the way here? Or if a bit of swank was demanded, why not Highgate? Venice, *La Serenissima*, was for losing yourself in the crowd, not for being part of one. Not to mention the cost: half the punters turning up today certainly couldn't afford the fare from England, so Stella would have stumped up. He did the calculations in his head. Not much change from twenty grand. What a waste.

Never mind. They were here now, he supposed. Onwards. Do the job and get out.

When he landed they were indeed all there, the survivors at any rate. He counted a baker's dozen, the old poetry crowd from the old poetry days, the roaring boys and girls, still game for a last round, blinking in the sharp autumn sunlight, some unsteady of gait, some already pissed and others wearing a thin blanket of carefully nursed resentment at their unsuccess, all trailing along the path among the headstones and sepulchres, past Stravinsky and Diaghilev and Pound, and finally assembling at the site of the interment in the district of the island where other forgotten poets had found their place and been overrun and consumed by ivy and yew.

Duveen, at Stella's request, was the MC for the occasion. Of course, there was really nobody else to fill the role. He had gravitas, and he could still speak in sentences. Once more he counted and then recounted the members of the interment party. Stella had asked him – 'Because I'll have my hands full, darling, as it were, with the ashes' – to make sure that the same number of people left as had arrived – though, on the other hand, what the hell? Who'd miss them? He counted again. He was always counting – syllables, stresses, audiences, sexual encounters, money: it all added up. People, if they noticed his counting habit, were curious. Why did he do it? Was it OCD? God, no. It was, well, it was something to do in the meantime.

Time to begin. Years of poetry readings (five hundred and twenty-six at the last count) had enabled him to speak to audiences while thinking about something else. It seemed to him now, as he talked warmly of the late Benedict Slattery and (stretching a point) his poetic achievements, that there should be a long service medal for people in the poetry game. He might suggest this to the Royal Society of Literature. The gong would have an image of Homer on one side and on the other of fingertips clinging to a cliff-edge. Actually, better to have three grades of award: The HRHS (Had to Read Him at School), The VHT (Vaguely Heard of Them), and the TO (Total Oblivion). 'Benedict Slattery,' Duveen went on fluently, needing no notes, 'had been a significant figure – not least for his strangely unread translation of Dante's *Inferno* – indeed, among the foremost… seventeen poets of a strangely neglected generation who were now in critical limbo and must look to the uncertain literary afterlife for their due.' There were some uncomfortable smiles at this.

He was probably pushing it a bit, Duveen thought, but what the hell? He had long since ceased to care: as the song said, *Roll 'em, smoke 'em, put another line out,* and the Devil take the hindmost. *Duveen, you're a rake,* thought Duveen. *You've had every woman here, if memory serves, part of a total of 193. Just don't expect any gratitude.*

Noon passed. A cold breeze came off the lagoon and through the trees. Duveen moved on to invite a succession of people to reminisce or read poems by or about the deceased. This was by turns boring and embarrassing. He concentrated on appearing to listen with appreciative nods and wry grimaces to the distended and almost incoherent anecdote attempted by Bernard Dingwall. The old twat should really have been in a home, or a cage, or preferably a box with his name on a brass plate screwed to the lid. But this too would pass. Try as he might, even Dingwall could not go crapping on forever.

And at last with a boulevardier's smirk, Dingwall gave way to Dinah Bacon. Poetry's glamour girl of 1968 was scrawny now, her skirt still too short and her ghastly bangles clinking as she waved her arms about in that actressy way, like a senile schoolgirl. Duveen had slept with her on an Arts Council tour of the Midlands – in Coalville, was it? And so, he believed, had the deceased, but then Benedict Slattery had slept with anyone and anything with the possible exception of street furniture and the dead. When Dinah seemed to have chattered herself to a finish, Duveen intervened suavely to introduce the next speaker. Whoever said life was short was talking bollocks.

Eventually it was Stella's turn. Flanked by her bodyguard of daughters, she took off her sunglasses and began to speak. Duveen realised that for her this was a state occasion. She was Dido on the Carthaginian shore, Jackie Kennedy at Arlington, Mme Mitterrand and her husband's mistress at the graveside at Jarnac, with Old Mother Riley thrown in for good measure. Stella had survived, no, triumphed, and she had seen off Benedict Slattery and was here to do him honour when he could no longer do anything about it, the poor short-arsed ginger bastard.

People would have paid money to witness such deafening restraint and thickly underlined dignity. The marriage, the love, the struggles, her sacrifices, Benedict's triumph, the loss of Benedict, the grief, the return to the stage in a provincial production of the *Oresteia*, in which she played Clytemnestra. Good stuff. Seventeen minutes and eleven seconds.

Duveen wondered how much of a performance it had been when Stella had first slept with him – (9 minutes 23 seconds) in Macclesfield, was it? – while Benedict Slattery had been on a writers' retreat in Galway; or when a little while later without warning she had offered to leave Slattery and bring her three daughters to live with Duveen, for feck's sake; or when, after he had declined this alarming offer in order, as he put it, ho ho, 'to save your marriage', not to mention Duveen's bank account, she took an overdose from which she miraculously recovered and then had started writing the illustrated children's books (twenty-six so far) that made her a fortune of her own, which Duveen would have found handy to access had he known how things would fall out. Did Stella in fact know when she meant it and when she was merely performing it? Did she care?

Though Duveen had indicated a Barkis-like willingness to reconsider the position in the light of these developments, she had never again suggested that they start a new life together. Indeed, their intimacy had faded, then lapsed and become a matter of nodded hellos across the crowds at publishers' parties. Now, he supposed, it was too late. Shame. And yet, she had rung and asked him here today to act as Master of Ceremonies. It would mean a lot to her. There was no one else she could rely on. Which must count for something. Maybe a bunk-up back at the hotel, take the edge off the widow's grief. Actually, forget the maybe.

Now Stella looked up and gazed across, and as if by a secret signal she and the daughters all smiled blindingly at him, before she went on to thank him as a loyal friend to her husband, herself and her wonderful family (here indicating the girls), which she had long considered him to be a part of. Effortlessly she disguised what must be the galling fact that for some reason Duveen was Slattery's sole executor, while referring with approval to what Duveen had hoped would remain a secret between Duveen and the publisher – that he was also to be Slattery's biographer. Duveen gave a modest shrug. Well, he thought, if you put it like that I must sound like a right cnut. In for a penny.

Stella completed her remarks and Duveen invited those attending to place poems in the urn, after which the party began its snail's pace return to the landing-stage.

'Very nicely conducted. Well done, Patrick,' whispered Dingwall, the condescending old shit.

'Not fucking amateur hour, is it?' said Duveen, counting the mourners once again to be sure. It was time for a drink. Five minutes back to the hotel,

Stella, followed by her daughters, fell into step with him as they walked back to the entrance.

'You did very well, Patrick,' she said, taking his arm.

'As did you, my dear. And the Three Graces here set the whole thing off to great effect.' The girls made no comment.

Stella paused and searched in her handbag. She produced a silver flask.

'Christ, I need a bracer,' she said. Her eyes were moist. Duveen felt a remote pity but put it aside. 'After you.' She offered the flask.

'Oh, no –'

'I insist. For old times' sake, Patrick. You made such a good job of directing the proceedings. And after all, you are one of us, really, aren't you?' The girls crowded in affectionately.

'Then *slainte*, my darling,' said Duveen. He took a good mouthful. Vodka, a herby sort. He'd always had Stella down as a gin girl. He handed back the flask.

One of the daughters rested a hand on his shoulder.

'Sorry, Uncle Patrick,' she said. 'Stone in my shoe. He turned and let her lean on him while she tipped an invisible speck out of her black stiletto. Talk about the princess and the feckin pea. Still, she had nice legs. All of them did. They got that from the mother. Legs up to her oxters, that one. When he turned back to Stella her handbag was closed once more and she was looking at her watch. Ten to three.

'Do say you'll be joining us for refreshments at the hotel, Patrick,' she said.

'I will, Stella, of course, but I've arranged my own transport. Need a little time to reflect. You understand.'

'Oh, I do,' said Stella, with a promising smile.

'Ooh, posh,' said one of the girls with a grin. 'You can see he's a poet.' To tell the truth he could never tell the daughters apart – Niamh, Marie, Bridget. How on earth had that ginger midget Slattery contrived to father these lissom black-Irish beauties? Maybe, thought Duveen, seeing as I'm family, I could exercise a little droit de seigneur in these parts. He looked up from these reflections. The women were nowhere to be seen.

When Duveen heard the waterbus pulling away from the jetty, he texted for his own boat to come and pick him up.

It was not dusk yet, but there was that slight enrichment of the light that marks its approach. He felt an agreeable melancholy. The old life, the poetry game, was almost done – the books written, the prizes won and the backs stabbed. In truth Duveen had long found it rather boring. So, wrap up Slattery's biography, complete with most of the dirt, claim the second half of the advance, and he could fuck off back to Narbonne and read crime novels in peace and award himself the odd *poule* for good behaviour. The ripeness is all, he thought. Last man standing, more or less. The great thing about vanity is that when you tend it properly it becomes invulnerable, he thought, as I am here to demonstrate.

He wondered where he would himself be laid to rest. He definitely wanted a burial – earth to earth, dust to dust, leisurely decay, none of this feckin cremation malarkey. Somebody would have to see to that in due course. It would probably fall to Mme Rocheteau, his housekeeper back in Narbonne. Bury me within range of the cathedral bells, that I may hear the tidings of resurrection. But don't do it just yet, Mme, not until we've had lunch and a siesta on that wide white shady bed of yours. The small death before the main course. But first things first: back to the hotel, then see to Stella.

Forty minutes had somehow mysteriously elapsed. At the jetty there was no sign of his boat, though surely he had made his requirements clear. He tried to ring the firm but now there was no signal. It was getting a bit late. There was a faint indefiniteness to the distances that had been clear an hour ago. There was a distinct chill. He paced a little, counting the seconds, too fast irritated, then after a time he paused and leaned against a wall, slightly breathless. This was not like him. He found a bench and sat. He looked at his watch but somehow his vision was blurred and he found his thoughts could not collect themselves properly. There was no one about. *Ridiculous*, said the voice in his head. *You couldn't make it up.*

When he awoke, Duveen's mind was clearer. It was cold now, and dark. Fog rolled across the black water. There was a sense of wide distance all around. The fog billowed and parted stealthily, opening momentary lanes into the lagoon and then sealing them off again. He was sure they'd left the city behind. He tried to sit up from the deep, musky-smelling cushions. In the prow hung a dim lantern. Duveen looked round. He was in a gondola. A gondola, for feck's sake. Should be a fucking motor boat. What were they playing at? Cheapskates. He turned to the oarsman, whose face was masked by the hood of an anorak.

'Where are we?'

'Not far now.' The figure spoke in heavily accented English, gasping a little as if suffering from emphysema.

'That's not what I asked. I need to go to the Hotel Accademia in San Polo. Take me there.'

'It is not far now.'

'Then where are we?'

'We are close. You should sit back, Dottore. Enjoy your ride.'

'But it's not what I asked for. They're expecting me at the hotel.' His watch was missing. 'What time is it?'

The gondolier shrugged and bent once more to his task. *After all*, thought Duveen, *what can I do? I've no idea where we are or where we'll end up or whose idea this stunt was. If I have a crack at the oarsman I'll most likely lose and end up in the drink.* He lit a cigarette and sat back.

Presently reed-beds and mudbanks began to appear. The gondolier, not slowing, steered the craft along a sinuous channel. There was a sudden appalling stench. Duveen was at a loss to describe it. You could go blind from breathing it, he thought.

The fog thinned a little and momentarily the lamp in the prow was answered by a faint one somewhere ahead. The reed-banks came closer and the boat slid along the noisome trench until it came to rest at the foot of the steps leading up to a jetty. Thirteen steps.

'Is this it?' said Duveen. 'You must be joking. This is bloody nowhere.' He turned. He still could not see the oarsman's face, but there were faint reddish sparks where the eyes must be, and Duveen found he did not want to look any longer. Canto IV of the *Inferno* lines 79-81 came into his head and he spoke them aloud:

> 'Non sanza prima far grande aggirata,
> vennimo in parte dove il nocchier forte
> "Usciteci" grido: "qui e l'intrata."'

Or, in Slattery's rather run-of-the-mill translation:

> 'We seemed to circumnavigate the place
> Before the ferryman came into shore.
> "Here is your stop. Now disembark."'

'Usciteci,' echoed the oarsman in that half-drowned voice. 'Get out. This is the place.'

You must play the thing out, thought Duveen. *Play the game. Play the hand you are dealt. It's a game, a literary game, a performance.* He climbed out of the boat on to the steps and walked up to the top. Fog and darkness, into which the jetty extended.

'Now what?' he said, and looked back. The gondola was already moving swiftly away into the night. After the last muffled sound of the oar, silence fell. Duveen walked along the jetty for some time. 159 steps. At last the fog parted and he made out a building ahead, a grim, castellated mass, with a gateway lit by two smoking torches. As he drew nearer his eyes were drawn up to the battlements where the three girls stood with their hair swarming in the windless air. Then he looked down again to where Stella appeared in the gateway. Her face in the torchlight displayed the impersonal fury of a goddess scorned.

'There you are, Patrick,' she said.

'So what's the drill, Stella, my darling?' he asked. 'This is a bit theatrical, even by your standards.'

At a signal from Stella the Furies began to descend the dark currents of the air, their inky locks swaying and hissing, and their gaze exultant. He counted them for luck, though he already knew the answer. 'Now, then, ladies,' he said. 'The Eumenides, I presume.' The girls alighted before him and approached, looking snakier by the second.

Later, much later, Duveen awoke once more, sealed in what he knew was a stone coffin buried upside down (the punishment for corrupt members of the priesthood, which in a sense he supposed he was; see *Inferno* Canto VIII) in what he had learned was the mausoleum of a leper house on one of the outer islands. He had to admit the list of charges laid against him was pretty extensive, and that it covered most of the main sins and some he'd scarcely heard of, and that there was nothing much to be said in mitigation, and that what he did offer had tended to make things worse from the point of view of agonising pain, torment and so on. So there it was.

But never let it be said that Patrick Duveen was not a trier. With his burning hand he reached into his burning pocket and took out his mobile. The dark fires illuminated the screen, but this, like the rest of the device, had turned to stone. So there was still no service. Best to try again in a bit. He started counting.

A Cold Spot

Everyone remembers a last really hot summer. Mine was many years ago – hot, but grey and sweaty east coast weather for the most part. My parents were divorcing, slowly and unpleasantly, and I knew I'd get nothing done at home, so I accepted my aunt's invitation and got the train out to Ellaby. Summer extended before me. I would give myself up to work and return to college ready to deal seriously with Part Two. The Long Essay was the main thing. I was writing about free will in *Macbeth*, a well-trodden path, but interesting. I had also recently broken up with a girlfriend I'd had since I was in the sixth form. It was a difficult time, but there was nothing to do except get on with things.

Ellaby was still just about a village in those days, but the city was stealing steadily closer across the fields. The older residents firmly continued to refer to 'the village' and 'the town'. Ellaby felt like elsewhere, if you know what I mean; comfortingly remote, with its little boat-builder's yard at the Haven, and the low, wooded ridge behind the park, on which stood further lines of grand, impractical many-floored, many-windowed, many-turreted nineteenth-century houses in dark brick, occupied by trawler-owners from the city.

My Aunt Jane, then in her sixties but still palely pretty, owned a large Victorian house beside the park, close to the river. Inherited from her parents, it was much too big for her, the family said, though they loved visiting it and hoped to possess it themselves in due course. In my view she was quite capable of leaving the place to the cats' home, and was quite entitled to do so, but I felt the attraction of the dark red brick, and pointed dormers, its slightly odd right-angled shape, and its position, sheltered from the river's weather behind a hedge and a row of poplars.

Aunt Jane had never married. She had been engaged, but all I knew about her fiancé was that he had died during the war. The waters had closed over this passage of family history, as over so many others. *Never you mind* was my mother's usual response to enquiries.

The house managed to be light and roomy yet somehow narrow and brown at the same time. Aunt Jane showed me up to the top floor. I had never penetrated so far upstairs until then. When I was a child there had been a locked door and I was told that beyond it was an attic full of junk. Now the door stood open and we climbed to a bare distempered landing with a skylight. To one side was an open door, to the other a corridor angled dimly away. Aunt Jane led me through the door. There was a double bed, a desk, an armchair and a view over the river. From here the water seemed very wide. 'Make yourself comfortable,' she said. 'There's a bathroom down the passage, and beyond that is a box-room full of books you might want to sort through for me. Keep what you like and we'll take the rest for jumble.' This was an instruction. 'I'll go down and put the kettle on. After that, well, don't think you have to spend time with me. I know you're busy. It's just nice to have you on the premises.'

She smiled, as though understanding my neglect in advance. I had the impression she'd spent much of her life waiting for something. On her sideboard was a picture of a handsome fair-haired young man – barely older than me – in RAF uniform, beside one of Aunt Jane as a WAAF. She was blonde and more than pretty, voluptuous almost, a little like Susannah York. Unthinkably long ago, ended but not over.

When she had offered me the use of the top floor to work in over the holiday, she said it would mean a bit of company for her – 'a man about', as she put it, and a lot of peace and quiet for me.

'This is very kind of you, Aunt Jane,' I said.

'Nonsense. Come down when you're ready.'

I put a few books on the desk, with pens and paper, and upended my holdall on the bed. That seemed to be it for unpacking. When I went out on to the landing its white bareness and inbetween-ness struck me. It felt like a sort of waiting-room, and it seemed both airless and colder than the rest of the house. It took a slight effort to take the few steps needed to go into the bathroom and look round and then go on down the corridor to the dim box-room with its Victorian trove of novels and histories neatly shelved and awaiting disposal. I had always been susceptible to atmosphere, or I had always created it: a back garden, an empty park at dusk, even the cellar of my mother's house, had all been places of fear. These days I managed, mostly, to ignore the residue of such feelings. Life might prove impractical otherwise.

Duty done, I went downstairs and my stay at Aunt Jane's got under way. We ate cheese on toast, a treat from childhood, not allowed at home, and afterwards we watched television. She noticed that I was preoccupied.

'What is it, Christopher?'

I shrugged.

'Oh, I see. You've noticed. Not everyone does.'

'On the landing?'

'Yes, dear, it's a cold spot.'

'Pardon me?'

'That's what they're called. Older houses have them sometimes. Does it bother you?'

'Not really,' I lied. 'I noticed it, but that's all. What does it mean?'

'Hard to say. It's just an uneasy place in a house, a cold place – like the patches of cold you get when you're swimming in the sea. You were always a sensitive boy. Would you rather not stay up there?' Whether or not this was intended as a challenge, I took it as such.

'Don't worry about me, Aunt Jane.'

'As you wish, dear.' She turned back to the screen. I went out for a walk along the river. It was tidal a long way inland. That evening the water was low, the mudbanks uncovered, slick, grey-brown and dank-smelling, with grey streams draining into each other down seams in the mud. A pair of swans eyed me from close in. As I went slowly along the footpath I saw two girls a way off on the grass, mooching along arm in arm. They seemed vaguely familiar. For some reason they lent the scene a melancholy remoteness, like something that had taken place long before.

When I returned and went up to my room, the long day was just beginning to fade, and a chalky half-moon looked in through the skylight. Was there anything, there on the white landing with the slightly rickety banister above the narrow stairwell? Something and nothing. A sort of patient alertness, perhaps. A cold attention. Always a sensitive boy. I went into the bathroom and cleaned my teeth, then crossed the landing and shut the door behind me. I was very soon asleep.

In the days that followed, when I looked down from my bedroom window I would see Aunt Jane, weather permitting, kneeling at a flowerbed in her blue spotted headscarf, trowelling and pruning. There was the slow sound of rain-interrupted cricket from the park, and the slow sight of barges heading upriver. It was a perfect place to read and begin to write my long essay. Although it was quite difficult to concentrate – it was summer, to be lived outdoors despite the muggy weather – I was quite disciplined. In the mornings I would walk to the river, then come back and work. Then came lunch with Aunt Jane and more work. In the evenings I would take another walk, this time to the Ferryboat Inn.

For once I didn't want company. My ex-girlfriend soon discovered my whereabouts and sent me letters drenched in perfume, their contents alternating between nostalgia and fury. I too was angry with her, but it didn't stop the waves of desire that broke over me at every unguarded moment. There was someone new in the offing, she said: so there. Perhaps this would make me come to my senses. A few pints dampened the discomfort. It was good to be elsewhere and then to be a little further out as well.

We were almost at midsummer when Aunt Jane announced that she'd be away for the weekend at a college reunion in Harrogate. 'There's plenty of food in the fridge. And I'm sure you'll be sensible about having the place to yourself.' I carried her case down to the station for her late on Friday afternoon. By 7 o'clock I was down at the Ferryboat Inn, a copy of *Macbeth* unopened on the bench beside me.

It was a long time since there'd been a ferry, but the pub did a steady, quiet trade. It was easier to survive back then. There were usually a few village lads playing bar billiards, and a few ancient solitaries nursing pints of mild. If it was dry, I liked to go and sit outside and watch the light shifting on the evening tide as the water reclaimed the mudbanks and the little tributary, the Haven where the boatyard stood.

'Got a light, Mister?' Two girls had appeared. My heart managed to sink and lighten simultaneously. Of course I should have known them the other evening in the distance. The blonde was Leah, her dark friend – the one I immediately thought of as mine – was Steph. They'd both played witches in a production of *Macbeth*, put on jointly by our schools. I'd had the rather unrewarding role of Malcolm, an accountant having to raise his game. Now, I'd heard, Leah was training as a teacher and Steph as a librarian. They'd been a gleeful, mischievous, flirtatious pair

– more fun in retrospect than my rather tight-arsed girlfriend Lizzie, who lacked conviction as the Third Witch. It was hard to imagine Leah and Steph (or me, come to that) moving on to respectable employment, or to believe that three years had passed since we'd performed The Play. They sat on either side of me in their denim jackets, white t-shirts and miniskirts. They were, as we used to say, dead lairy.

'We took you for a gentleman,' said Leah.

'You're not going to disappoint us, are you?' Steph asked.

I lit their cigarettes and then fetched them vodka and cokes.

'We heard you were around,' said Leah. 'Staying with your auntie.'

'I wonder how.'

'Lizzie's given you the chuck,' said Steph.

'Sort of.'

'No, I mean, that was the message she wanted us to give you. You're chucked.'

'You sound like fourth-formers. Anyway, all that's over and done weeks ago.'

Steph shook her dark curls and grinned, 'Not according to her. She wants you to suffer.'

'A lot,' said Leah. 'Loads.' They both cackled.

'Well, I suppose I am suffering. I've come here to get away.'

'But there's no escape, is there?' said Leah, stroking my hair.

'Lizzie's got another bloke,' said Steph.

'I know.'

'Bet you don't know who,' said Leah.

'I couldn't care less.'

'It's only Thor Andersen,' they said in chorus and collapsed in choking laughter.

'What, that plank? You're fucking joking.' Thor Andersen was an amiable moron, son of a trawler owner, possessor of an

MG sports car and no 'O' levels.

'I don't think it's his mind she's after,' said Steph.

'Perhaps you couldn't meet her needs,' said Leah.

'You're a nasty pair of cows, aren't you?' They nodded.

'But we're on your side, aren't we, Leah?'

'We never liked Lizzie. She's a boot,' added Leah. 'And she was crap at being a witch. But we like you, don't we, Steph?'

'Oh aye. Ever so.' When they approached I'd put the book in my jacket pocket. Now Steph removed it.

'Speak of the Devil,' she said.

'It's work,' I said. 'For an essay.'

'Don't be a dull boy,' said Leah. 'It's the holidays.'

'I've got to catch up. It's been a difficult year.' It was starting to rain, a drizzly, sweaty rain that would set in for the night. 'I'd better get back.' They rose and took an arm each.

'Where are we going?' said Steph.

'*I'm* going back to my aunt's.' I made to detach myself. They held on.

'She's away, isn't she?' said Leah.

'How do you know that?'

'There are no secrets in Ellaby. In the Twilight Zone.' It was a bad idea. Leah and Steph had obviously had a drink before they showed up, and they seemed a bit stoned too. But their cajolery was flattering and I realised with a pang that it would feel lonely without them. So in they came. Then they wanted something to drink, so I searched in the kitchen and found most of a bottle of gin and issued a memo to myself to replace it the next day. By this time they were in my aunt's sitting room.

'Don't touch anything,' I said, without conviction. Leah picked up the photograph of Aunt Jane from the sideboard.

'Is this your aunt? Look at this, Steph. She was really beautiful back then, wasn't she?'

'Mmm,' agreed Steph. 'So who's the feller? Looks like a film star.'

'Her fiancé.'

'What was he called?'

'I've no idea.' Steph tutted at this.

'Got to do your research.'

'What happened to them?' said Leah.

'He died during the war. He was a pilot.' The girls looked at each other, moved by the story that suggested itself in this spinsterish house.

'So he died when he was young,' said Leah, 'and thinking of her as she was then, but all this time she's been getting older, so he might not even recognise her at first sight. Imagine that.'

'And she never married. She's stayed true to him,' said Steph. She shook her head. 'That's really sad, isn't it?' Leah was suddenly restless.

'Let's see the rest of the house,' she said, going back into the hall. We went upstairs.

'Smells of old lady. Lavender and that,' said Leah, wrinkling her nose.

'More like death, ask me,' Steph snorted, shrugging off the feelings of a minute ago.

'Don't be rude. I'm very fond of my aunt.'

Leah halted us when we got to the landing. It was dim and blue in the rain-light, the white walls seeming to glow a little.

'Woo. Feel that,' she said. 'Can you feel it, Leah?' Leah nodded.

'Feels cold.'

'It's an old house. It's a bit damp,' I said. Now they were standing at the wall opposite the bedroom door, stroking the powdery white surface.

'Creepy,' said Steph. They turned from the blank white wall and looked at me. 'Do you know about this?' I shrugged. 'I mean, you can feel it, can't you?' she insisted.

'Even you, a mere man, lacking our feminine insight,' said Leah, with a grin.

'Yes,' I said. 'I can feel it.'

'Well, it's better than watching Val Doonican.'

'It's a cold spot, according to my aunt.'

'So what does it do?' Steph asked.

'I don't think it does anything. I think it's just there.'

'It's dead creepy. Perhaps you'll have to protect us.'

'Perhaps he won't have his shirt on,' said Leah. 'And perhaps our clothes will be revealingly torn and we'll have to climb up an iron ladder through the flames to safety.'

'But one of us will fall. And will he catch her? You never know. What do you think, Christopher?' said Steph.

'Shall we go in and have a drink?' I asked, feeling heavily outnumbered. 'This way.' I led the way to the box-room.

'There's nowhere to sit,' said Leah, looking round.

'I'll get some cushions,' I said. 'Wait here.' But of course they came with me across the landing and into the bedroom.

'This is more like it,' Steph said. 'Don't worry – you're safe with us.'

To begin with, though, the bedroom was a bit of an anti-climax. The girls sat on the high bed, swinging their legs and passing the bottle between them. The rain thickened and the room darkened. The night would be uncomfortably warm.

After a while, Leah said, 'So what's this about *Macbeth*, then?'

'I'm writing an essay on it over the summer.'

'Aren't you sick of it? You must know it backwards. We both do, even now.'

'No, it's the play that excites me most.'

'What's your essay about, then?' asked Stephanie, taking a sip of gin and passing the bottle to Leah.

'Free will.'

'How do you mean?'

'Does Macbeth perform his crimes of his own free will, or is he compelled to commit them by powers larger than himself?'

'I think he's free,' said Leah. Steph nodded, slightly groggily.

'Yeah. Otherwise what's the story?'

'I would have agreed with you, but when you get to the end don't you think it looks as if every step he took was inevitable? His soliloquy might seem to suggest that.'

'Suppose,' said Steph, slightly bored. 'Does it matter?'

'So it's the witches who set him off,' said Leah.

'Maybe. "You secret black and midnight hags".'

'Watch it. Hey, let's do a scene.'

'We'd need three witches,' said Steph, lying back sleepily. But Leah was insistent.

'Chris can be a witch too. Go on – it'll be a laugh.' Steph shook her head and sat up.

'Which scene, then?' asked Steph.

'The one where they're waiting for Macbeth and Banquo to get there after the battle.'

'The opening of Act One, Scene Three,' I said.

'I dunno if I can remember it,' said Steph. She was clearly drunk now. Leah took the bottle from her, drank from it and offered it to me.

'Yes, you can. You will once we get started.'

'Can't we just read it?'

'Better to act it. Get off the book, as Mr Whatsit used to say. Chris is Third Witch and prompter – not that we'll need it – and stage directions. And us two'll do the sound effects, the thunder. Come on, stand up, Steph.' I made to put the light on but Leah shook her head. 'There's enough light. It's more atmospheric in the gloaming.'

We formed a rough circle.

'Let's do it once as a warm-up, then do it as if we mean it,' said Leah. She looked at me and I opened the book and nodded for them to begin. The first time through was more or less accurate but a bit wooden and hesitant, and Leah, the First Witch, nudged Steph to make her concentrate.

'All right,' I said. 'Once more with feeling.'

Having recaptured the exultant, menacing energy they'd given off on stage, the girls collapsed, giggling. I took a drink and offered them the bottle and they passed it between them, rolling their eyes at what they'd done. No one said anything for a minute or two. The discharge of energy seemed to have left us all a bit flat and uneasy, as if we'd lost something. The rain grew heavier against the dim window. After a while, Leah announced, 'I need a wee,' and went out, closing the door behind her. Maybe I felt a faint draught then, as though the landing breathed out.

Steph came over to the armchair where I had collapsed, lowered herself on to my knee and without any announcement started to kiss me. I liked Steph kissing me and she smelt nice and was quite curvy. I gave myself up to this unexpected development and it must have been several minutes before she drew her head away and looked round. 'Leah's been gone a long while,' she said. I shrugged and Steph, suddenly sober, stood up and said, 'I'll just go and make sure she's all right, hasn't been sick or something.' She went out and I rose and looked out of the window at the near-dark. There was the siren of a vessel out on the river.

A minute later Steph came back.

'She's not there, Chris.'

'Eh?'

The bathroom was open and she wasn't there, and I went to the box-room and she wasn't there either.'

'Would she have gone home?'

'Her bag's still here. She wouldn't leave it. She wasn't pissed.'

'Well, she likes a laugh. Maybe she's hiding.'

'Don't be daft.'

'Or didn't want to play gooseberry. Or maybe she's poking about downstairs.' We went out on to the landing. When I tried to switch the light on it fused. The dim space flattened and absorbed our voices when we called Leah's name. We checked the bathroom and the box-room. Nothing. Then we searched all the rooms downstairs.

'Well, she must have gone home and forgotten her bag.'

'No, she wouldn't, I told you,' Steph hissed. 'She's staying with her parents. We should ring.'

'It's too late for that.' It was midnight. 'There's no point in worrying them.'

'Well, we have to do something. Come on.' So we walked down to the Ferryboat and then along the river path and back over the railway bridge. The rain had slackened off and high tide brushed at the low river-wall. No sign. At a loss, I walked Steph round to her parents' house and we agreed to speak in the morning. There was no kissing this time. Back at my aunt's house, I stood on the dark landing, waiting and listening. It seemed to me that the tension had left the place, that the alertness had been replaced by sleep. But who could I tell that to, and what would it have meant to them?

Leah was found two days later, washed up on a mudbank in the mouth of the Haven, fully clothed except for her shoes and with no marks of deliberate injury. Steph and I were questioned at length. The police seemed most interested in the idea that there were drugs involved, having found traces of cannabis in Leah's bloodstream. But there was nothing to go on, and Steph and I were clearly as shocked as anyone else.

The coroner's verdict was death by misadventure. The summer ended with this village tragedy and ensuing scandal. My aunt was stoical but, I thought, intensely embarrassed. I went back to college. Steph and I never met again, and having no good reason to visit Ellaby I let contact with my aunt lapse.

Ten years later, I was asked to visit Aunt Jane in the nursing home at Ellaby. The house had long been sold, and now, I was given to understand, her time was short. I admit I went unwillingly: what on earth could we talk about? When I arrived she was wrapped up warmly, waiting in a wheelchair in the hallway. She was pale and tiny, and her eyes had that look of someone already half-departed.

'Christopher, I would like you to take me for a walk along the river,' she said, quietly but firmly. Off we went, over the railway bridge and along the riverside path. Downriver I could see that new estates had almost reached the Haven. The village of Ellaby was done with. After a while Aunt Jane indicated that we should stop at a bench. The water was low that afternoon, with a lightship heeled over on its chains on one of the big banks near the deep channel. Clouds raced seaward. There were swans on the shore.

'I need to tell you something,' said Aunt Jane. 'I need you to hear a confession. Can you do that for me?' What choice did I have? I nodded. 'As you know,' she went on, 'I was engaged to be married once, during the war. To a bomber pilot, training to fly Lancasters and then stationed at the old RAF base across the river at Kevington. He was called James, and I was deeply in love with him. You remember his photograph. He was very handsome and very loyal.' She paused. 'There are a great many sentimental things said about those times, about romance and the intensity of life when violent death was very possible, but I know that for us there was truth in them.' Pain passed across her face, and she reached for my hand. 'I'm a silly old woman, Christopher.'

'Never, Aunt Jane,' I said, and found my voice thickening.

'And you're a good boy. But I need to get on with my story… On what turned out to be his last leave, James and I went to bed together. People did that, you know, even then! But it was the first time for us. And afterwards he told me to stay in the bedroom – your room, that was, up in the attic – because he would hate to say goodbye at the door and just wanted to get off and anyway he'd be back soon enough. And I tried to do as he asked, but I couldn't, and I went out on to the landing after him and called to him as he went down the stairs. I said that if anything happened to him I would not be able to live, and that I would kill myself, throw myself in the river. And though this was a foolish thing to say, I did mean it, and I could tell James believed me, from his expression when he paused on the stairs and looked back at me and gave a nod and told me to go and put some clothes on. He believed I wouldn't live without him. I had made a vow, there on the landing.

'A week later his plane was badly damaged in a raid over Holland. He managed to get back across the North Sea, but he had to ditch in the mouth of the river. None of the crew survived. I thought I would die, of course, that I would kill myself, but time went by and I didn't. I told myself there was work to do for the war effort, that there were bigger things than me or my feelings, that James wouldn't really have wanted me to die.

'So I survived. I never married, never looked at another man, went on living in the old house, living with the memory of James and hoping this kind of fidelity was enough. But it wasn't, was it?' She shook her head, refusing to weep. 'It wasn't enough, because I'd promised, I'd made a vow. And I'd betrayed a dead man, the man who was my lover. He never had the chance to grow old, as I did: for him I would always be young and pretty, and always breaking my promise. So there, gradually, was the cold spot, all that coldness and waiting, there on the landing.' I opened my mouth to argue, but she gave me a sharp look. 'Of course, this isn't information of a sort I could have given to the police. They'd have ignored me or sent for a psychiatrist, wouldn't they? And no wonder. But it's true. I know it is. And I can tell you do as well. Your friend, that pretty blonde girl, Leah, poor silly thing, that's what happened to her, isn't it? James grew tired of waiting and then one night there she was, and the promise had to be fulfilled.' Aunt Jane squeezed my hand. I found I had no reply. 'And then, I suppose, I was free, in a way.'

We sat for a while looking out at the river, the glittering grey banks with the light driven over them beneath the hurrying clouds. The swans had disappeared. Soon it was too cold to stay.

Revenant

MACKLIN WAS HIMSELF ALREADY on the chilly station concourse, watching the train he'd arrived on pull away again, when the producer's assistant texted him that their train was delayed. He understood. Everything had always delayed its arrival in this town as long as possible – Cuban-heeled boots, miniskirts, drugs – because it was that kind of place, the end of the line, or, he thought, in this context, the line-ending. He might be able to use that in the recording. He made a note as he stood in the cold archway looking out irresolutely into the street for a little while, feeling old.

There was no one much about, though it was a Monday morning. He had time, so he made himself set off and walked around the old town. There was the matt aluminium sky he had known in fact and memory all his life. The marina and the inner docks were almost empty. He made for the marketplace. It was not market day, and the bare stalls with their plastic awnings looked temporary, standing on the cobbles in front of St Edward's. The bells were ringing the hour. The cathedral church had never been cleaned of its encrusted smoke and grime. It was portentous and unforgiving, gazing coldly down from its grey heights as if knowing him of old.

He went inside and sat in a pew near the back, breathing the smell that was partly chill and candle wax and partly the passage of time. In his mind's eye a long-dead Bishop was addressing the schools service on Remembrance Day. His theme was 'I'm All Right, Jack'. Macklin allowed his attention to drift, and he spotted her again, her dark hair under the dark red of the beret swinging as she turned to whisper to the blonde girl sitting next to her, the hissing look of the schoolmistress at the end of the row, the girl's unrepentant grin as she turned and caught his eye and held his gaze. Nothing had changed, then. Afterwards he would lose her in the crowd and be too nervous of seeming foolish to try to find her among the other girls talking in groups as they dispersed to their various buses. And anyway, what would he have said? *I like your hat? I like your hair? Fancy a coffee at the Kardomah?*

Macklin emerged from his reverie. He had dreamed of the girl the previous night, out of the blue, after years of giving her barely a thought. She was going upstairs. It was a party somewhere off the park, but there didn't seem to be anyone there. She wore a red minidress and, like many of the girls that long-ago autumn, a black velvet choker. Where the stair turned, she looked back down towards the hallway where he stood, as if searching for him in the crowd. But there was no crowd. She moved out of sight and he began to follow, but, as is the way of dreams, his intentions had no purchase. Now the stairs led out into the park, and he walked beside the pond, along a path deep in leaves, until he came to the entrance to the palm-house, when he awoke. Macklin rarely remembered dreams, but on the train he had retraced his steps several times through this one. It must be the thought of coming back. How long since last time? Ten years and more. Since he finished the biography of the poet Maurice Ashover. After that there was no need. He had no one of his own here. Friendships had lapsed and times had changed.

Two workmen came into the church and began hammering. Macklin walked back to the station. It was only 10am and yet it was remarkable how dark it was. The girl in the beret and later the red dress, she and all the other girls, where had they gone? He looked at the arrivals board. There was still time for a coffee, so he went into the Railway Hotel and sat in the foyer beside a pillar with a plaque bearing a quotation from a poem by Maurice Ashover: *'No one comes here. No one leaves. / By night the bell of the lightship grieves.'* This, it seemed to Macklin, must be a bit dispiriting from a hotelier's point of view, but such was the posthumous fame of the poet that the whole city was studded with plaques bearing quotations from his work, each more gloom-inducing than the last. *And*, thought Macklin, *I'm meant to be a fan, insofar as a biographer can be. God knows what the unpersuaded make of it, supposing they even notice.*

There was a statue of Ashover on the station concourse, caught in motion, rushing for a train, arm raised as if in (wholly uncharacteristic) greeting. Although Ashover was dead, he had exhausted Macklin, who in the course of writing the biography moved from the instinctive affinity he had felt since he first read Ashover's poetry in his teens, through dislike of its limitless yet limiting pessimism, and finally to a bloodless indifference which coloured his sense of nearly everything, and from which, he suspected, as he closed in on the age of sixty, he would not now recover. He was exhausted, like a creature colonised by another. His own poetry had simply ceased. Ashover's was better – no, it was *stronger*. If you believed in the Oedipal struggle against the anxiety of influence (see Bloom, Harold, 1973), Macklin had been vanquished, transformed into an epigone, a repository of innumerable lines from the Ashover oeuvre. The anxiety of effluence. His head was full of earworms. Everything from the night sky to an empty milk bottle displaced him in favour of Ashover's sonorous gloom.

'You must be Francis.' Macklin looked up. Two women with small wheeled cases stood before him. He must have nodded off. He got up.

'Sorry. Yes, hello. It's Frank, actually.'

'Frank,' said the older and taller of the pair, 'this is Jemima, my programme assistant. And I'm Beverley. Thanks for coming.'

'It's home ground,' Macklin said.

'But you don't live here now, though?' said Jemima, looking from him to her notebook and back.

'I find you never really get away.'

'And Ashover would have agreed with you, of course,' said Beverley.

'And you're a poet yourself,' said Jemima. 'Not just a biographer.'

Thank you for telling me, thought Macklin, and made no reply. It was a moot point: how long did you have to be silent in order for people to stop referring to you as a poet? Was there such a thing as an ex-poet?

'I've hired a car,' said Beverley, 'so shall we make a start?'

They drove down to the pier, the setting for Ashover's most famous poem, the one about the ferry leaving in the fog: *'We fear it won't come back/ And that there is no other side,/ A gap instead, a world away, a lifetime wide.'*

They went back up the river to the ancient Jewish graveyard by the docks, where the poet had often walked. Macklin guided them down the tangle of streets into the legal district, glancing in at the offices of the firm of solicitors where Ashover had worked and The Hanging Judge, the pub where he spent the increasingly long afternoons which eventually met up with the evenings at around the time he was able to afford to give up paid employment and do his drinking at home in the attic flat. They looked at the quotation from Ashover displayed in his favourite corner. In these places they recorded Macklin's observations on the work, and at Beverley's insistence, the life. *I am so boring,* Macklin thought. *I must sound like old paper whispering to itself.*

Beverley looked at her watch.

'Jemima and I need to be off to London by five,' she said. 'So let's press on. Where next?'

★

'Err nerr, never,' said the receptionist at the private hospital where Ashover had died.

'Really? No one ever enquires about him?' asked Beverley, with the patient smile that Macklin was already growing to dislike.

'Err nerr. Nerbody. Was it important?'

'We're making a radio programme,' said Beverley.

'For Radio 3,' said Jemima.

The receptionist remained blank.

'The BBC,' Jemima prompted.

'And this gentleman you're looking for, you think he's a patient.'

'Was,' said Macklin. 'Was a patient.'

'He died,' said Jemima, nodding. Macklin wanted to slap her.

'Well in that case he won't be here.'

'In 1982,' said Macklin.

'Err nerr. We don't, you know, keep them,' said the receptionist, glancing longingly at the phone as though it must ring and save her.

'Understandably. The place would soon be full to bursting,' said Macklin.

'OK... Well, you know the plaque?' said Beverley.

'Nerr. If it's plaque, you want the dentist's, not us,' said the receptionist, more confident of the ground now.

'No, the *plaque* on the outside of the building.'

'Err nerr.'

'Would you like to come and take a look at it with us and tell us what you think.'

'Nerr, you're all right, thanks.'

They regrouped outside and considered the plaque and its inscription from the poet's last completed work. '

'This place, this place – it's like walking into one of Ashover's bloody poems,' said Beverley. She asked Macklin to read aloud the lines on the plaque.

'I'd rather not,' he said.

'But there's no recording of it we can use otherwise,' said Beverley, her smile a rebuke. Macklin did as he was asked. *The road runs out into a track, a path, a turning/ Leading nowhere. Now it smells of burning.'* Then he did it again, exactly the same but apparently better.

'So what must the poet have been feeling when he wrote this?' Beverley asked.

'I've no idea,' said Macklin.

'Despair? Resignation?' Beverley prompted.

'Constipation?' said Macklin. 'Although people do it all the time, it's a mistake to identify the poem with the author and his or her experience. Poetry is an art, not simply testimony.'

'But you must admit, there are obvious links here.'

'Why must I?'

'Because that's what the fucking programme's about. And in case you've forgotten, you're a biographer, which is why we're here. Shall we try again?'

Macklin conceded the point. He didn't want to be there all day.

In the car park, Jemima listened back to the recording of the encounter with the receptionist.

'I suppose we might find something to use from that,' she said, without conviction.

'Well, there's Sophie Kingsmead coming into the studio tomorrow,' said Beverley. 'So at least that's something.'

'I didn't know she was involved,' said Macklin. He had

188

been asked to devise the programme, only to see it altered in almost every respect. 'What's her... contribution?'

'Oh, cultural context. You know. Reputation. Gender and so on,' said Beverley.

'A more contemporary view,' said Jemima.

What am I, then, thought Macklin, *dead?* He could see where this was heading. Ashover would be found wanting before the court of contemporary attitudes. As usual. *Fuck the lot of them.* Macklin resisted the temptation to simply leave. He was just too tired to make the effort. He was sick of Ashover but he couldn't let go.

His attention wandered to the Dutch-fronted house opposite. It was partly obscured by a large Victorian fountain in the street, featuring large-breasted mermaids, recently repainted in bilious khaki. They had formerly been a deep, much preferable green. And the house beyond – someone whose name he'd forgotten had lived in the first-floor flat, and the girl was a friend of a friend, and they'd been there one afternoon with a few others, smoking dope and listening to music in a back room overlooking the long garden and the orchard. It was late autumn.

'Come with me,' said the girl. They slipped away from the others and went down into the garden. The lawn was covered in frozen leaves.

'I want to see where it ends,' she said, and leaned on his shoulder so that she could take off her high heels.

'You'll ruin your tights. You'll catch your death,' he said.

'Come on.' She went ahead, up over the parterre, then vanished among the trees. Macklin looked back towards the house. He saw a figure at the attic window gazing down. Was the gaze regretful? Forbidding? Proprietorial? The onlooker was too far away to tell with certainty, but given the address it was definitely Ashover. It must have been not long before he left the flat. Beginning of the late period. Drink taken, as Macklin now knew with considerable precision from his research. At the time he said nothing to the girl, judging that to have read Ashover's work and know he lived in the attic might not help his cause – not that the cause seemed to be his exactly.

He surfaced now hearing the bells of St Jude's.

'Onwards,' said Beverley. 'Where next?'

'Eh? Sorry. The flat, I suppose,' said Macklin, aware that both women were staring at him. 'It's only over the road.' How long had he been under, this time?

Mrs Pizarro, the landlady, was in her mid-eighties but still spry enough to welcome visitors.

'Mr Ashover was up the top all while he was at the solicitors,' she said. 'It was only when he got famous that he thought he should buy a house of his own. I advised him against it – I mean, what was the need? – but I suppose really he had no one to please beside himself. I suppose it was something for him to do. Not that it did him any good. Eighteen months and he ended up across the road there in the hospital. Anyway, it's empty up there in his flat now. Bring the key back down with you. I'll put the kettle on.'

They trooped upstairs. Beverley opened the door of the flat. Chill and damp breathed out. There was no furniture. Ancient red lino covered the floor and the walls were dotted with lighter patches where pictures had been hung.

'So the room with the garden view would be through here,' Jemima said. Down the corridor an open doorway led into the famous study. Here Ashover had done his best work, twenty years of it, at a desk before a tall, arched window that opened onto a balcony with a low stone parapet. All of which had got into the poems one way or another, though Macklin was of course determined to deny the directness of the connection between the place and the poems.

'So, Professor Macklin, what does this spartan setting tell us about Ashover?' asked Beverley.

Macklin forbore to say: *That he's not here. That he's dead.* 'It's a place for solitary concentration and contemplation. The garden view itself has become famous over the years because of the poem associated with it. "Down the Path" – though of course the poem is a work of the imagination.'

'But the imagination has to start somewhere.'

'I think it may be more complicated than that,' said Macklin.

'Well, let's hear an extract,' said Beverley, keeping the irritation out of her voice, and indicating a page in the *Collected Poems* with lines asterisked.

From memory Macklin recited:

'She leads him down the path, away into the trees.
Few are the days, and fewer the nights
That ache as dark as these.
The leaves are down, the guy is burnt,
And after all the love and death
No lessons have been learnt
For still she leads him down the path
Away into the trees.'

'Again, please,' said Beverley.

As he repeated the stanza, Macklin felt afresh how poisonously sentimental these lines might seem if one were disposed to find them so, and yet how addictive. They seemed to leave a metallic, bloody taste in his mouth.

He turned back to the window and looked out and down. Fog was rising from the frosty floor of the orchard, and the far end of the garden could not be seen. He felt as if something had been stolen from him. It was from here that Ashover had looked down as Macklin and the girl began to make their way through the trees. And from that view arose the poem: *'For still she leads him down the path / Away into the trees.'*

Beyond the long orchard, concealed by laurel bushes and encircled by a path, was a round pool on whose far side stood a summerhouse. They had gone there. The door opened with a damp creak. Inside was a wickerwork chair.

'Sit down,' she said. He did as he was told, and she perched on his knee.

'So we've arrived,' she said. *Yes*, he thought, *but where?'*

'Aren't you cold?' he asked.

'You can keep me warm,' she said. She leaned in, kissed him and put her tongue in his mouth. 'You're right,' she said after a while. 'My tights are ruined. I might as well take them off.'

'Well, we should get going,' said Beverley, in the bright voice used with the old and mad.

Macklin struggled to focus. *Which was the present tense?*

'I'd better go and have a cup of tea with Mrs Pizarro, to thank her,' said Macklin. 'If you don't need me any more.'

'As you wish.'

'When will you want me in the studio?' Macklin asked.

'Studio,' said Jemima, as if this were an unfamiliar concept.

'We'll be in touch,' said Beverley. 'Do thank Mrs... er... for us.'

I see, thought Macklin, as he watched the women drive away. I have made myself surplus to requirements. It wouldn't take all that much to replace his contribution to the programme. There were newer biographies by newer biographers, revisionists and theorists eager for the opportunity to be heard by whoever it was that listened to this kind of thing, a demographic of which Macklin himself had ceased to be a member some time before. He couldn't in fact think what it was he did do in the evenings. In fact, he couldn't remember the evenings at all. He turned and knocked on the door of Mrs Pizarro's flat.

'This poetry,' Mrs Pizarro said, as they sat in her kitchen drinking tea and looking down the garden, 'it doesn't make you happy, does it?'

'Ashover wasn't happy, no. Quite the contrary.'

'Too much in your head. You can't live all in your head, can you?'

'You may be right.'

'I don't know why he couldn't lead a normal life. Family and so on. I suppose some folks just aren't made for it.'

'That's true,' said Macklin. An immense weariness flowed through him. He could quite happily have been scattered there and then like ash in the wind, a burnt page that might never have been.

Mrs Pizarro gave him a careful look.

'And what about you?'

'What about me?'

'It's not too late, you know.'

'For what?'

'Find a nice girl, son. Have a bit of fun. You know the song?' She began to sing in a grainy contralto:

> You better have some fun
> You ain't gonna live forever
> Before you're old and gray, feel okay
> Have your little fun, son!
> Have a little fun!

Macklin found himself walking up the drive of the hotel on the park with no sense of how he had got there. He checked in and went to his room, where he sat on the edge of the bed. It was a clear, cold evening, with the moon a little past the full. Before he went under again, it struck him that spells like this must be like the offstage lives of characters in fiction: nothing doing, no conversation, a marked absence of the fun which Mrs Pizarro had commended him to have. *The half-life of fiction*, was his last thought.

He waited in the street under a lime tree until Mrs Pizarro's lights were out, then slipped through the gate and along the side of the house into the garden. At the edge of the lawn he stopped and listened and looked up at the dark house, at Ashover's attic window. *'The cold was bitter, the frost already hard, / The full moon frank in its detached regard.'* *What is it with me,* Macklin wondered, *when my every second thought seems to be a quotation from Ashover? But let the story tell itself,* he added, and moved on through the freezing night, across the parterre and into the wood that glittered with frost. She would not be there. She was long ago.

He expected that everything would have changed, that he would be dismissed from this involuntary fool's errand. But there was the pool, and beyond it the summerhouse with its door ajar as the pair of them must have left it in the penultimate decade of the last century, with the idle smell of dope and the ruby glint of the stone on the girl's choker. Could this, at last, be an assignation?

Macklin waited in the freezing summerhouse. There were times when he was lost to himself – he could tell by the altered position of the moon. He was being consumed, like a store of material. There were the bells at St Jude's again. He felt himself draining away. But he would see it through: there was no choice; he was an element in a larger conception. Someone, even now, was making him up. He was being dreamed by a dead man. So there was no reason to suppose the girl would come, though he could see her stepping lightly over the frozen leaves, her shoes in her hand, her red dress too thin in the cold, her grin a shameless challenge. Ashover's lines came unbidden to his mouth. She was *'all the beauty he will ever know. / Where then, where then, where did she go?'* *Resist,* he thought, *for once. For once, speak your own words.* But he could remember nothing of his own. Instead he found himself singing an ancient song that Ashover would have viewed with exact and fathomless contempt. *'So you wait, you wait and wait/ Girl don't come.'*

Far away a light came on in the attic. *The song must carry on the night air,* thought Macklin, and that was that. There was no pool and no girl, no Macklin either.

A Green Shade

SUMMER, WHEN AT LAST it came, was in earnest. Overnight the Dene was crowded with leaves and blossom. The twisting paths seemed steeper and more ambiguous in the flickering shade, more secretive with promises. The stream in the valley floor had deepened and grown stately, gliding over the rocks it tinted in tea and gold. Overnight it came to feel as if it had always been summer, and that this is where they had all been headed – the good place that lay on the other side of exams and marking, the good place which extended indefinitely, off the calendar and off the clock, the place behind the waterfall, the invulnerable pastoral to which it now seemed the leering statue of the satyr by the bridge in the Dene had always been pointing. Now it made sense to put on The Play, thought Francis Webster. The stars were aligned, the forecast good. Time for a last hurrah before retirement.

When the matter had been raised, at the end of a staff meeting back in January, it was announced by Guy Todd, the new Head of Department, that The Play could not be staged on university premises for reasons of Health and Safety. There were questions of insurance and the risk of lawsuits. Someone must have mentioned the accident that had occurred during rehearsals of *Love's Labour's Lost* the previous year, when the Princess of France had accidentally pushed the King of Navarre off the stage and into A&E. It could have happened to anyone, but that, according to Health and Safety, was the point. What is life without risk? asked Webster. Non-litigious, came Todd's reply. So there would be no staff-student play this year, it seemed. And anyway, that time could surely be more usefully spent on open days and grant applications.

Webster, like one or two other older members of staff, could remember that the tradition of The Play had been long established when they themselves arrived as junior lecturers in the remote past, when admin had been the province of one endlessly accommodating secretary, and when pleasure was seen as a vital accompaniment to the serious work of teaching and research. Surely The Play could not be permitted simply to die and go the way of Old Norse and Practical Criticism. The death of The Play was only a symptom of the larger process or transformation – or, as they thought of it, decay – which would soon make their beloved institution unrecognisable and inhospitable. Webster was of retirement age. Others younger than him were being shown the wisdom of calling it a day before they were pushed. They could see the writing, or rather the PowerPoint, on the wall. And they, like Webster and his Chair in Renaissance Studies, would not be replaced.

Renaissance Studies, his lifelong passion, an entire three-dimensional world of learning and imagination, where science met pagan mysteries, and where gods and philosophers walked the passageways of power, was to be 'slimmed down'. This was proposed by Guy Todd. Todd was the smiler with the knife beneath the cloak, agent of the Business Studies wolves who were ransacking the university entire. Shakespeare would be studied in 'contemporary' forms, i.e. without all that poetry. Todd's own 'thing', apart from his small guitar and to the extent that his administrative duties allowed or even made it desirable for him to have 'a thing', was post-Buffy Theory. But Todd's Mission Vision, or whatever he was calling it, was of a merger with Media and Communications. 'Let's make English useful again!' was his motto.

'You don't know what you're playing with,' Webster said,

after Todd had laid out his plans at a meeting which left several staff in tears of impotent range.

'It's not a game, Francis,' said Todd, with a smile that many people hoped would one day prove fatal. 'We, that is the university, have to position ourselves in world terms.' He fingered the small guitar to which he often turned when pretending to think.

'By enabling the students to remain in the semi-literate condition in which they arrive?' asked Webster.

'That's a very narrow view. The view from an arrow-slit. Come down from your ivory tower on Mount Olympus.'

Come in and get me, copper, thought Webster.

'And join you in the general morass?' was what he said.

'Now you just sound bitter,' said Todd, rising to signal an end to the meeting. 'Anyway, after the summer none of this will concern you.'

'As an Emeritus Professor, I will still have an office.'

'Ah, yes, that's something else I should have mentioned. We're having to rationalise the use of space. Best all round really if you could clear your stuff as soon as possible – in your own time, of course.'

And so the future welcomed the staff with open talons. Later, from his office window, Webster watched Todd, resplendent in his Hi-Vis Lycra poncing suit, ride off into the night astride his expensive and evil-looking bicycle, small guitar case containing small guitar strapped to his back.

'I told you, Todd, you've no idea what you're playing with,' said Webster, turning to consider four walls of books and numerous additional piles of them, and a lifetime of paper accumulated on every other surface – all to be cleared 'in his own time as soon as possible'. What Todd could not understand was that the Renaissance was not a dryasdust bolthole for allegedly 'irrelevant' scholarship, but the gateway to the larger, permanent reality framed by Shakespeare and his contemporaries. Then, as Webster always did when sorely tried, he went to call on Araminta. The beautiful and mysterious Araminta, the long-serving Administrator of the Department, who knew everything, all the secrets and shortcuts and scandals, had run the place with ironclad graciousness and a sense of power in reserve, until Todd had contrived her removal on the grounds of age at the end of the previous autumn term. Even in retirement Minty, as Webster alone was permitted to call her, might have an idea of how to proceed in what Webster called the War Against the Yahoos. It seemed to Webster that Minty had been biding her time.

Araminta poured him one her special gin fizzes.

'It's time for Lord Pybus,' she said. They raised their glasses in a toast.

And now summer had come. And there would be The Play.

'We have three weeks,' said Webster to the half-dozen people who showed up for the lunchtime meeting down in the sunlit Dene.

'And no play,' someone said. 'Is this going to take long? I'm being assessed by Human Resources this afternoon. I think they plan to extract my mineral content.'

'And even if we had a play, there's nowhere to put it on,' said someone else. 'And there are plenty of other things to worry about. Like the merger.'

'We can stage the performance in Lord Pybus's Ground,' said Webster.

'I don't even know where that is.'

'Didn't I read in the bulletin that they're planning to sell it off?'

'Yes, but not yet,' said Webster, patiently.

Lord Pybus's Ground was a walled enclave within the Dene itself. It had been given in perpetuity to the university by the eponymous Lord Pybus when the place was newly founded in the late nineteenth century – as a pleasure garden, to be used for 'contemplation, solitary study and seasonal entertainments'. Lord Pybus, the last of a line stretching back into the late Middle Ages, had been an aesthete and literary dilettante. He had deliberately looked backward in framing these terms of reference. But two world wars and the post-war expansion of Higher Education and all the rest of it had left the pleasure garden increasingly unvisited. These days, God knows, there was little enough time for contemplation. And of course, the university was naturally keen to monetise the site (for nothing can be left simply to be itself) and property developers were keen to help in this process. The Business School's lawyers were working to undo the terms of the bequest, in order to bring Lord Pybus's grounds under the same regulation as the rest of the university. But that would be later, when summer was over. Summer was now, fully charged with green promise. There was time, still, to put on The Play.

'How do we get the use of the place?' someone asked. 'How do we get in?'

'Like this,' said Webster. 'He produced a heavy iron key, redolent of dungeons and councils of state and beheadings at dawn.

'How did you get hold of that?'

'Araminta passed it on to me when she retired at Christmas. She thought it might prove useful. She told me that the other copies seem to have been mislaid over the years. So we have exclusive access to Lord Pybus's grounds in order to put on the play.'

'Don't we need permission?'

'No.'

'But Guy Todd said Health and Safety said –'

'The terms of Lord Pybus's bequest stipulated that his grounds should be used in perpetuity for entertainments. So how can I put this? Health and Safety can, as it were, fuck off.'

Nervous laughter. Surely Health and Safety were not there to be mocked, any more than God had been in his day.

Webster pressed on.

'Power comes from the barrel of a gun, or, in this case, the barrel of a key.' He struck off from the main path, and the others followed, content to be entertained. Presently they came to a high wall in which was a narrow, barred gate. On the lintel lines of verse were carved:

> Annihilating all that's made
> To a green thought in a green shade.

'Amen to that,' someone said.

Through the bars they could see a deep glade with some kind of wooden structure half-visible on the far side of it.

'Shall we go in?' said Webster. The key moved stiffly in the lock. 'Before we do so I must swear you all to secrecy. This will be a private performance, with an invited audience. Is that understood?' The others looked baffled. 'I'll take that as consent.' They trooped through the gate and Webster locked it behind them.

'As you can see,' Webster said, when they emerged from the wood, 'there is already a stage for us to use.' A paved area with a few rows of old-fashioned metal folding chairs ended at the low stage projecting from a small proscenium box theatre made of lath and plaster and decorated with faded classical figures of satyrs and maidens.

'There were concerts held here, and plays were staged, and masques,' said Webster. 'A specially written masque was performed here during the Festival of Britain in 1951. And it is a masque that we shall be performing, but something of an older date, not a modern attempt at recreation like Coghill or Empson.'

'You mean Ben Jonson?'

'Contemporary with him. *The Masque of Wisdom.* Written in 1611 by the then Lord Pybus, and performed at midsummer here or hereabouts for an audience of the local nobility. It is an allegorical work.'

'It sounds very… edifying,' said someone, doubtfully.

'Oh, it is, believe me,' said Webster. 'I have copies with me, so we can read it through now while we eat our sandwiches. It's quite short.'

'You know my views,' said Todd, 'and those of the university.'

'As I have explained,' said Webster, 'and setting aside the fact that I too am of the university, the regulations governing Lord Pybus's grounds are different from those applied to the rest of the university estate. But Guy, what I wanted to say was that we should not part on bad terms. It will send a positive and transparent signal to the rest of the Department if you are seen to be happy to attend the performance. It will show the wisdom of co-operation and collective endeavour as the Department moves into a challenging phase of change and development.'

Todd stared at him.

'You're serious about this, aren't you?'

'Always. And if you will accept the advice of an old man, you would be wise to accept the invitation to attend The Play. To attend as a welcome guest, to show the staff that you really are one of them, and help persuade them that you have the interests of the Department at heart.'

'I must admit,' said Todd, 'I'd like to see inside Pybus's Grounds before we – they – build on it.'

'Well, then,' said Webster.

'Very well,' said Todd.

'So we have a truce?' Webster asked. 'For one night only? And would you bring your guitar?'

'My guitar?'

'Yes, we may invite you to give a song during the

performance. The material is up to you. I'm sure an experienced performer like yourself would not be intimidated by such an occasion. Or am I wrong?'

Todd laughed tolerantly. 'Show me the stage and I'll do the rest, matey.'

'Till soon, then, matey. And by the way,' said Webster, 'let's keep this between ourselves. Give the troops a surprise on the night.'

'Say no more,' said Todd, with his most odious smile.

Araminta poured Webster another of her special gin fizzes.

'He called me "matey",' said Webster. 'Honestly, Minty, I had to stop myself from punching him.'

'All in due time,' said Araminta. 'You've given him a reason to turn up.'

Guy Todd did not ask for a copy of the script and Webster did not offer him one. Todd was busy in committees and with playing his small guitar. When the two men passed in the corridor, Todd would give a thumbs up and make strumming gestures. Webster, for his part, would wink in what he hoped was a conspiratorial manner. Meanwhile he pressed on with recruiting the cast and holding rehearsals. As he had known would be the case, the students from the Drama Society were keen to take part, especially with the promise of a party in the mysterious Pybus's Ground afterwards – and the sense of being on the inside of a secret, a conspiracy. The secrecy was deafening.

The summer held, rich with heat and light, like a promise yet to be broken, green–gold in the evenings where he put the actors through their paces on their light, fantastic feet.

On Midsummer's Eve the performance of *The Masque of Wisdom* was preceded by a buffet supper of bread and cheese, olives and rough sea-dark wine served to the audience of past and present staff and friends, including the resplendent Araminta, by members of the cast already costumed as satyrs and (anachronism be damned) nymphs, who would then form the chorus for the masque. Webster himself poured Todd, who had chosen to wear a leather jacket, the wine of welcome and made sure that he and his small guitar were seated in the front row, next to Araminta.

This done, the actors slipped away among the trees while the rest of the audience took their seats. A drum roll. Lights came up and the stage was shown decorated to seem continuous with the woodland setting. A pipe sounded and the chorus of nymphs and fauns entered and performed a dance of welcome. Then the ancient sage Silenus came forward, wreathed in vine leaves and carrying a book. He was accompanied by two goat-horned satyrs.

Satyr 1
Who owns this ground where none may go?
Silenus
The one whom all should fear to know.

Satyr 2
Why trespass where we may not be?
Silenus
Because its master summons me.

Satyr 1
Say what's in your master's mind.

Silenus
I bring a book that must be signed,
The sum of all philosophy,
Of what has been and what must be

Satyr 2
What of your master? Who is he?

Silenus
Those who are not blind shall see.
Lord of limit, lord of light
And of Hades' endless night,
Wine god, sober god of laws,
The end of all, the primal cause,
The prince of ambiguity.

Satyr 1
So many names! Who may he be?

Chorus
The god's a blade, a suit of flame,
The rule that rules the only game.
If it is wisdom you desire,
Wiser far not to enquire.
But hark – the great lord now draws near.
Attend we him in love and fear.

There was a blare of brass and Apollo, clothed in gold, masked
with the sun, appeared, lowered to the stage on a wooden
platform. The stage now grew dark but for the light that
surrounded him. The Chorus cried out in awe and terror.

Apollo
The god Apollo: I am he.
Who is it dares to summon me?

Silenus
I, my lord, at your command,
And this sportive sylvan band.

Apollo
Silenus! Well met, ancient sage.

Silenus
My lord, accept this humble page
Where all that time can teach this age

Is written, and we now request
You put its wisdom to the test.

Apollo
Then give the book to me to con.
Let music play! I'll speak anon.

Apollo now retired to consider whether the document containing the sum of all philosophy and learning was acceptable to his divine understanding. This was the signal to begin the antimasque, an interlude with music and dancing, during which by tradition an important member of the audience might be induced to join the performance. The nymphs descended from the stage and invited Todd to rise and join them. They whirled him in a ring-dance, then led him on to the stage. He seemed a little groggy.

'Drowsy syrops,' said Araminta. 'Can't go wrong with them.'

The small guitar was placed in Todd's hands, and Silenus came forward.

Silenus
Music is the god's first love.
So must you hope he will approve
The minstrelsy you offer up
And grant you his ambrosial cup.

Todd seemed to recover himself. He bowed and came to the edge of the stage, from where he began to deliver an alleged song that even Webster recognised as being by a popular beat combo of the day. Considered as music, it sounded like a pregnant cow being tormented with electrodes in an empty swimming bath, but it was clear that Todd himself was pretty impressed by it. Eventually the yowling ended and he took a further deep bow which was rewarded with a smattering of official-sounding applause. Then, as Todd made to step down from the stage, the two satyrs seized and pinioned him while a nymph removed his small guitar. Silenus appeared once more.

Silenus
Unhappy mortal, you must wait
Until the god decides your fate.

The platform bearing the god descended once more, his sun-mask enlarged. He brandished the book. When he dismounted, two nymphs placed the platform upright. It stood revealed as a rectangular frame six feet in height, with straps at each corner. Todd looked anxiously around, but he knew enough not to come out of role. Apollo turned to address him as the satyrs bound him to the frame.

Apollo
Wretched overweening creature,
Todd by name and turd by nature
I am everything you see:
The world in which you've lived is me –
And in my world there cannot be
Triumphant triviality.
This nonsense which you claim is song
Is always and forever wrong.
Marsyas, when he challenged me,
Could rival me in minstrelsy.
I liked the music that he played
Yet nonetheless I had him flayed.
–Take this one hence. Are knives supplied?

Chorus
Yes! Hail Phoebus Apollo! Yes!

Apollo
Then let the satyrs have his hide.
Let this Olympian butchery
A warning to all mortals be.

Chorus
Apollo! Dionysos! Apollo! Dionysos!
Aiiiieeeee!

The frame, with Todd struggling against his bonds now, was drawn up out of sight.

Apollo
Now, Silenus, wise old friend
Our last performance nears its end,
And here upon your humble page is
Truth enough for seven ages.
Blood and death gave beauty birth –
And that is all ye know on earth.
You disbelievers who presume
Apollo's safely in the tomb,
Oh never trespass on my lawn:
You'll wish that you had not been born.
Now, nymphs and satyrs, bid good night.
Take off your masks and dim the light.

There followed an explosion of blinding brightness followed by a thunderclap. When the smoke cleared the stage was empty. The audience rose in silence, uncertain quite what they had witnessed. Neither Webster nor Araminta was anywhere to be seen. And if the crowd heard the howls of agony from somewhere in the woods nearby, they preferred not to mention it, but went quietly back through the shadowy glade, out though the gate of Phoebus Apollo's Ground, and away to their cars and their lives in the slowly cooling darkness.

The Aspen Grove

A COUPLE OF TIMES a year the travellers would come with their trotting horses and sulkies and take over the big field by the pub for a few days. Morgan supposed they were preparing for competitive events, but he'd never bothered to find out. All he knew about was Appleby Horse Fair. That's to say, he knew it existed, in what used to be Westmoreland, and that various authorities, the council, the RSPCA and so on, wanted it shut down. It was part of the low intensity war between the Gorgios and the travellers. It was the ragged edge of things. Resistance could only have one outcome, and as such, he thought, it was akin to the various kinds of contemporary sentimentality – meditation, mindfulness, macramé (as he thought of them), and that daft form of martial arts where you spent months polishing an imaginary horse. Distractions. Away with distractions!

No one hereabouts seemed to mind. People, children especially, liked watching the horses and their riders going through their paces. The landlord liked their custom in the pub. Their visits seemed to be part of an informal local calendar, a custom, along with the Onion Johnnies coming over (in ever decreasing numbers) from Brittany on bikes, with sacks of onions to sell door to door, and the Pitmen's Derby up at the racecourse, when local women got dressed up like parodies of Ascot and came back shrieking drunk to argue with their menfolk and each other in the pub car park till all hours. Where did these habits come from?

Morgan reckoned he was indifferent to all this. He had his work. It was enough. When he needed distraction he took his walks over the big field and through the paddock to the graveyard. Or he took the newspapers to the pub and sat undisturbed in the lounge. Even after thirty years he was viewed with a slight wariness because of his different accent and the fact that he was obviously educated. People knew he wrote. He was said to have been working on a book for some years. Faced with his impermeable politeness on the topic, people had given up telling him that if they too had time on their hands like him they would also write books.

The years passed, the travellers and the Johnnies came and went, the womenfolk exploded in the pub car park, and Morgan stuck to his task.

It was believed, though there seemed to be no direct evidence, that it was also the travellers who periodically brought things to the paddock and left them there in the doorless tumbledown shed near the aspen grove that marked off the big field from the paddock and the graveyard – all kinds of stuff, including fridges, a sofa, a spin-dryer, a hallstand with a mirror, on one occasion a church pew. Local custom – that again – meant that anything left outdoors and visible was considered to be available to take away. Morgan himself, long ago, shortly after arriving in the city, had arranged for the council to take away a worn-out chaise longue, and been confronted by two irritable men with a council lorry and a demand for the ten pounds' removal fee. The chaise longue had vanished before the men arrived. Later that day Morgan spotted it in a neighbour's front room. They called this a custom. He knew what he called it.

But his outrage had long diminished. Now, when he saw a new consignment in the shed, he made a bet with himself about which items would be taken first. Settees, no matter how ancient and scarred, were always popular. Eventually everything would go and be replaced by one or two shaggy, depressed-looking horses, not designed for trotting, who would see out the winter, grazing on the long grey grass, apparently untended but with the use of the shed and an old bath they drank from. Then they would be gone too. The leaves would return to the grove of aspens, with their sound like falling rain. The graveyard continued to fill up.

This was the world, Morgan supposed – like a style of muted wallpaper he scarcely considered any more as he took his constitutional. Sometimes he might pause in the graveyard to disapprove of a particular headstone. It was carved to resemble the vertical striped shirt of the local football team. Then there were the bears. He would wonder if he dare remove the little bears and fairies and windmills and bits of washed-out plastic tat and other ghastly oddments which had begun to accumulate around the graves. It was like a re-emergence of paganism from the deathbed of the C of E. It was vulgar. But if he took something and binned it, someone would be sure to see, so he didn't.

The statue was different.

He didn't really see it at first, and had gone some way further down the path when he stopped, wondering what he had half-noticed. He went back. The statue stood near rather than inside the shed, on a slight tilt, one shoulder resting against the trunk of an aspen. There was a new lot of stuff in the shed – an ancient fruit machine, a stereogram from the sixties with a leg missing, a mangy moquette footstool, and one of those basket chairs that used to be suspended from the ceiling in advertisements in the 1960s, occupied (alas no longer) by kohl-eyed models in minidresses. Those were the days. Alas.

The statue had its back to him. *Her* back to him, it turned out when he got close enough for a proper look. She, the statue, was about five feet tall, white, made of stone. She had a white floor-length robe – a *chiton*, he remembered – drawn in at the waist. Her hair was bound at the temples, her arms by her side, her expression neutral, her wide white eyes sightless yet candid.

It took him a moment to adjust. She was, Morgan thought, a descendant of the women in that faintly improper strand of Victorian Hellenism that produced the paintings of Waterhouse and Lord Leighton and Sir Lawrence Alma-Tadema – R.A., thought Morgan scornfully. They might be nonsense but they existed to this day, 'languid and bitter-sweet', reclining as though forever, on marble terraces both real and imagined, high above the flat summer calm of the Aegean, waiting for something, though what that was remained undisclosed – the beating of oars or wings, as had been foretold, et cetera. Oh, yes, Morgan knew her and her kind. But, he decided, this was a goddess, or at least semi-divine, rather than mortal.

Curious that she should be here in this autumnal aspen grove, among the deceased white goods and other crap in this hoard of the temporarily abandoned. She must really belong in someone's garden on the fringe of the city, in one of the fake-posh suburbs, the aspiring locals traded up to only to find they'd arrived nowhere, while the incomers and other snobs had absented themselves and moved still further out. And someone had stolen this minor goddess and left her here in the grove, for the moment, before, presumably, she was collected and taken on to her new home, or dumped more permanently.

Interesting, thought Morgan, standing in the kitchen steeping a teabag until the liquid in the mug was almost black. From here he looked across the lawn to a fence, on the other side of which lay the pub, the car park, the big field separated from the paddock by the grove of aspens. He could picture the statue leaning against a tree – he had resisted the urge to set her upright. Clearly she didn't belong with all the other stuff. Someone might spot her and decide to take her for their garden before the gypsies came back.

Morgan had made his life simpler after the last girlfriend had finally given up and gone. Inherited money meant that, as a kindly old lawyer would inform an heiress when the will was read in a detective story, he could afford to please himself. He pleased himself by narrowing his range of contacts and renouncing his obligations. He gave up his position at the university, gave up book reviewing and poetry readings and all the rest of it. He switched his attention completely to prose and concentrated on the novel which had occupied him for seven years now.

The novel was not finished, nowhere near. If he had cared to tell anyone he would have said he was in the early stages of the middle, with an option for a detour back to the beginning. But Morgan no longer had that kind of conversation. Nor did he care to mention what it was about. In fact it was about a woman, or rather a composite of various women with whom he had been involved since his youth. Morgan had given up women as well as everything else. It didn't occur to him that this renunciation might have been reciprocal. He was trying to render in fiction the essence of what he thought of as the difficult sex. Many people, among them the women who'd tried to live with him, would have told him that 'essence' was an illusion. He preferred to differ. On he went page by page, migraine by migraine, the seasons rolling on into another. *At least I'm serious*, he thought.

He took the mug of tea upstairs and went to his desk. His study looked out over the fence on to the field and the aspen grove. He switched on the laptop but found himself trying to work out which of the aspen trees was propping up the statue. She, the statue, was not visible from here. Anyway. He opened the file of manuscript and began to read the previous day's work. Ordinarily, though he was generally speaking as unimpressed by his own work as by anyone else's, the task would absorb him instantly and for several hours. Now he could not apply himself properly. Decades of self-discipline failed him. For a terrible moment he thought he might switch on the television, then remembered that he'd got rid of it.

Half-past midnight. The revellers from the pub, who liked to gather in the car park for a last quarrel for the road, had finally dispersed. Morgan unbolted the gate and stepped out on to the back lane leading to the field, pushing before him a rather conspicuous two-wheeled upright yellow trolley. The noise of the wheels on the path seemed deafening. He waited for lights to come on in the houses. Then he was crossing the frozen ground and entering the grove. With a torch he located the statue and then wrestled her aboard the trolley and bound her in place. It was a long time since Morgan had been so excited. This felt like transgression, he thought, and yet it is only snobbery. Who would care about whether he or anyone else took the statue?

In the morning he placed the goddess in the shade of the jasmine bushes near the pool. This seemed to suit her. It looked as if she was silently emerging from the trees, perhaps intending to bathe. Good. She was a cut above the usual statuary. And she completed the garden, as if she had been missing before. Now he could look down on her from the desk at his study window. He was able to resume work on the book. But he still found himself pausing to gaze out at the immobile figure by the water. In her world, nothing would be changing; time would not be passing; the clamour of mortal preoccupations would fall on deaf ears. She might be petitioned, but she would show no pity. She was what she was, beyond judgement or alteration. *That's more like it*, thought Morgan. She was better than all that Victorian kitsch.

Then it came to him. She was not English but French: Eurydice as painted by Corot in 1856, being led out of the underworld through the woods to safety by her husband, the poet Orpheus. In one version of the story she had been bitten by a snake on her wedding day and plunged into the underworld. Orpheus descended to rescue her, on condition that he walked in front of her and did not on any account look back. But just before the couple re-emerged on earth Orpheus gave in to temptation and Eurydice sank back into Hades, beyond all saving.

It was just getting light when he heard sounds from below. He went to the study window. Through the open back gate – surely he hadn't left it open – he could see a green lorry with its engine running. Then there was movement on the lawn. He ran downstairs, out of the kitchen door and along the path. Someone had strapped the goddess back on to the trolley, cheeky bastard, and was starting to haul it towards the gate.

'What's your fucking game?' said Morgan. The figure with the trolley turned and looked at him. He was startled to see that it was a young woman, bulked out with a padded waterproof. 'You can't take that.'

'Not yours, Mister.' The accent was faintly foreign.

'I found it,' he said.

'Wasn't for moving,' she said. There was a noise. A second young woman appeared, similarly dressed. Both were dark-haired and sunburnt. They might be sisters.

'Out,' he said. 'Before I call the police.'

'You're the thief,' said the second, taller woman, resting a hand casually against the trellis.

'Everybody knows that you can take what you want from what's left in the shed,' he replied.

'Everything else, not this,' said the first woman, who

seemed merely to have paused and still meant to drag the trolley with her at any moment.

'Says who?'

The women laughed, but mirthlessly.

'You are a fool,' said the newcomer.

'This you don't understand,' said the woman with the trolley.

'If you wanted to sell the statue, you should have kept it somewhere else,' Morgan said, aware that he was speaking too loudly. He didn't want to attract the neighbours' attention.

'Not for sale,' said the one by the trellis.

'No. The statue is meant to stay where it was put, in the aspen grove,' said her sister. She took her hands off the trolley and turned away from him 'He is a fool. He cannot understand.' Her companion nodded and the pair of them moved off towards the gate.

'Don't come back,' said Morgan. 'Or I'll call the police. And the RSPCA would confiscate those horses – the state they're in.'

The women turned.

'This is a bad day for you, mister,' one said.

'You are to be pitied,' added the other.

And then they were gone, closing the gate behind them. Morgan made sure the gate was bolted. He listened as the lorry moved slowly away over the cobbles. He was shaking with fury. He had been accused, *accused* – but everyone knew the rules about things left out, in the lane, in the grove. Everyone knew.

Morgan had no interest in dreams, but that night they began to take an interest in him. He found himself walking through the ashy grove, where smoke and sulphurous fumes rose from the amaranth that covered the ground. The grove – he had never noticed before – tilted slightly downhill. After a time he came to the shed, but it was now a cave entrance from which a scorching breath came in gasps. He turned, vainly looking for the way back.

He woke at first light, dressed and went out into the garden. The statue was gone, as he had known it would be. Those women, he thought, as he opened the gate and set off across the field towards the grove, determined to see the place in the light of daylight reason. The place was different when he arrived. All the junk was gone and so were the horses. The aspen leaves chattered together in the frosty air. There was no birdsong. The statue had not been put back. He turned, irresolute.

Once more, the ability to work deserted him. For the thousandth time he made himself re-read the manuscript. It seemed to him a work of almost demented sterility: his application of blood, sweat, tears and irony had drained the life out of it. He remembered a musician saying that having taken drugs over an extended period he had come to feel as if he was listening to sculpture. Morgan's book, too, was stony. He took a sleeping pill.

Now he saw Eurydice among the aspens, a little way off, wandering as though lost. The air was darkening as he pursued her, gaining a little, then losing sight of the slim figure who moved so lightly over the smoking ground. If she would only look back, she would see him and consent to be saved. He could smell what seemed to be burning earth.

Shaken by the repetition and the development, he made a rare visit to the pub at lunchtime. He was the only customer. He sat with the paper, occasionally looking up to see the barmaid fiddling inscrutably with her mobile phone. She knew better than to talk to him, but for once he longed for conversation. Time crawled past. Eventually the darkness came. He sat at the window, unable to write or read or think, staring out at the dark field and the aspen grove.

With a choice of whisky and pills that night, he chose whisky.

The grove tilted more steeply now, and the smoke and fumes were so thick that sometimes he could barely see. In the air and underfoot the heat seemed to pulsate. The ashy leaves chattered more loudly and they seemed about to speak a language he could understand. He witnessed his own terror and despair as though he were merely one more object in the scene, and yet he felt that terror and despair with a choking directness he had not known was possible. He was lost. He was lost. How long he waited there he could not have said, while the heat intensified and the smoke thickened, and the birds came to the brink of speech.

Then he saw her, standing as when she had first encountered him, with her back turned. And yet now she extended a hand behind her, and he knew he must take it. The hand was cold. He held it; it did not hold him. And she led him away between the burning trees and through the gathering dark, while the birds grew deafening and the ground shook. For some time the pair walked uphill in this fashion. If he was Orpheus, he thought, should he not lead the way? But he was lost and she was not.

After an age, the darkness softened a little and he could see an arch of clear air between the trees. Beyond it sunlight was falling, and the horses stood among the discarded cookers and armchairs. It was closed now. He would be saved. She would save him. They went on a little further until between the trees he could see the gate to his garden. Home. Life.

It was only now that she turned, letting go of his hand, and looking at him directly for the first time. In the instant before he saw her face he supposed that now she would have human eyes, and would speak. But the face that met his gaze had the empty, candid, dispassionate eyes of the statue, and its expression did not alter in its ageless neutrality. Having looked, she turned away again and set off towards the arch, while Morgan, in the moments left to him as she passed through the arch and it was closed by curtains of smoke and flame, knew that he was turned to stone and that the stone would burn forever.

About the Author

Born in London, Sean O'Brien grew up in Hull and now lives in Newcastle upon Tyne. He is a poet, critic, editor, translator, playwright, broadcaster and novelist. His poetry has won multiple awards, including the T S Eliot Prize, the Forward Prize (three times), and the E M Forster Award. His eighth poetry collection, *The Beautiful Librarians*, won the 2015 Roehampton Poetry Prize. His second novel, *Once Again Assembled Here*, was published in 2016, as was *Hammersmith*, a chapbook of poetry and photographs. 2018 sees the publication of his ninth collection of poetry, *Europa*, and his second collection of short stories from Comma Press, *Quartier Perdu*. O'Brien is Professor of Creative Writing at Newcastle University, and a Fellow of the Royal Society of Literature.

ALSO BY SEAN O'BRIEN...

The Silence Room

ISBN: 9781905583171
£9.99

'Strange, creepy, often brilliant' – *The Financial Times*

'Darkly thrilling' – *The Independent*

Chain-smoking alcoholics, warring academics, gothic stalkers and aspiring writers are just some of the visitors that browse the mysterious library at the heart of Sean O'Brien's fiction debut. Idlers and idolisers alike can be referenced, in body or in text, among the crepuscular alcoves and dim staircases of this seemingly unassuming building. The secret to a family curse, a dog-eared first edition of Stevens' *Harmonium*, the gruesome fate of a feminist literary theorist – all are available to simply take down from the shelf, as are the myriad genres and subject areas that O'Brien himself masters: from gothic horror to English pastoral, Critical Theory to Cold War noir.

Take a walk between these shelves. Crack the spine and the blow the dust off lives unlived because, so far, they're unread. Become, if you dare, as trapped as them...

'Sean O'Brien, like Graham Greene, creates his own instantly recognisable fictional landscape, where crime, mystery and disillusion lurk by the waters of the Tyne or Humber. His stories glint with black comedy and touches of the macabre and surreal... First-class stories from one of our finest writers.'
– Helen Dunmore

Letters Home
Martyn Bedford

ISBN: 9781905583751
£9.99

'Martyn Bedford is the genuine article, a writer of unmistakable flair and accomplishment.' – *New York Times*

When an out-of-work actor discovers his bedsit once belonged to an obscure, suicidal painter, he turns his talents to re-creating the ultimate site-specific performance...

As a teenage girl drifts from depression into a permanent state of sleep, she becomes the focus of both scientific interest and an unexpected, cult following...

Against a backdrop of hooliganism and hostility, an asylum seeker writes letters home assuring his family how welcoming England is...

Many of the characters in Martyn Bedford's stories find themselves at a point of redefinition, trading in their old identity for something new. Whether it is an act of retreat or escape – fantasising about storming out of a thankless job, or just avoiding a bad-tempered husband for a few moments on Christmas day – they each understand the first step in changing a reality, is to reconstruct it.

'Haunting and intimate portraits of vividly different lives that get under your skin and stay there.' – Jeremy Dyson

The Ghost Who Bled
Gregory Norminton

ISBN: 9781905583560
£9.99

' Unfailingly beautiful, deceptively simple and
lyrically powerful.' – *Irish Times*

A simple act of gallantry in the Malaysian jungle spawns a
lifelong feud in the Home Counties...

A fading actor with a terminal illness devises a meticulous plan
to leave the stage in style...

A pregnant composer contemplates motherhood at the end of
civilisation...

Spanning centuries and continents, the stories in this collection
amount to a tour de force of literary worldbuilding. From
deeply insecure time travellers to medieval mystics and
futuristic body modification cults, Norminton's characters find
themselves torn between conflicting impulses – temptation
and fortitude, hubris and shame, longing and regret. By turns
sad, strange and darkly comic, *The Ghost Who Bled* reveals a
master storyteller of incredible range.

'Good fiction encourages us to look at the world from
another's perspective, and in his new short story collection,
Norminton explores this idea in extremis.' – *Guardian*